"What if we were not one person, but three in one body—created by careless gods who forgot to 'close the gate'? Akwaeke Emezi's novel, *Freshwater*, paints a fiercely unique, unforgettable story of identity, mental health and the world beyond ours. This impressive debut is lyrical and well-told."

—Tananarive Due, author of *Ghost Summer*

"A clarion call to those of us who find that our minds are more haunted and complex than that of the status quo. In exquisite, unearthly prose, Akwaeke Emezi renders the ordinary strange and the strange, ordinary—making *Freshwater* the most stunning debut novel I've read in years. An unforgettable literary experience."

—Esmé Weijun Wang, author of *The Border of Paradise*

"*Freshwater* is one of those dazzling novels that defies these kinds of descriptions. We can gesture to the story—set in Nigeria and America, told by all the selves of its Tamil/Igbo protagonist—but such synthesis fails to convey the magic that awaits its reader. At once fiction and memoir, potent in its spiritual richness and sexual frankness, the text seems not to have been written by but channeled through its brilliant author. This may be Emezi's debut novel but she is an old—an ancient—storyteller: thrillingly at home in the tradition of griots, poets, seers and seekers."

—Taiye Selasi, author of *Ghana Must Go*

Praise for *Freshwater*

A National Book Foundation 5 under 35 Honoree

Shortlisted for the Center for Fiction First Novel Prize

Longlisted for the Andrew Carnegie Medal for Excellence in Fiction

Longlisted for the Brooklyn Public Library Literary Prize

A *New York Times Book Review* Editors' Choice

"Akwaeke Emezi's bewitching and heart-rending *Freshwater* is a coming-of-age novel like no other . . . For anyone who has experienced life as a misfit or outcast, this is a resonant rendition . . . Potent and moving, knowing and strange, this is a powerful and irresistibly unsettling debut."

—David Wright, *Seattle Times*

"Akwaeke Emezi is a name you will want to remember . . . *Freshwater* is unlike any novel I have ever read. Its shape-shifting perspective is radical and innovative, twisting the narrative voices like the bones of a python. A novel so unique and fresh, it feels as if the medium has been reinvented." —Safa Jinje, *Toronto Star*

"A startling debut." —Katy Waldman, *New Yorker*

"A new kind of bildungsroman . . . *Freshwater* reimagines the genre of psychological self-portrait."

—Josephine Livingstone, *New Republic*

"Ground-shaking . . . It is a battle for a body and a soul, and the stakes are high." —Nadja Spiegelman, *Paris Review*

"The great trick of this novel is that we want not only peace for Ada, but also for the troubled spirits inhabiting, and one with, her.

Reading Emezi's unfolding integration of fictional forms and modes of thinking—spiritual, analytical, historical, cultural, clinical—you feel like you are witnessing a talented and emotionally astute writer finding her voice(s). *Freshwater* is a dazzling, problematic debut that promises so much more." —Rob Spillman, *Guernica*

"So shivery, so electric, that the first coherent thought you can put together as you read is that you're watching a major new talent beginning to carve out a space for herself . . . *Freshwater*, ultimately, is not a book about giving in to one's demons, but about living with them." —Constance Grady, *Vox*

"*Freshwater* is sheer perfection: sexy, sensual, spiritual, wise. One of the most dazzling debuts I've ever read."

—Taiye Selasi, *Guardian*

"Akwaeke Emezi parts the seas of the self in her engrossing debut novel, *Freshwater*." —Sloane Crosley, *Vanity Fair*

"Harrowing yet beautiful . . . Every sentence left me reeling, every paragraph on the edge of my seat, and every chapter begging for more. I could've spent hundreds of pages more in Emezi's lush creation . . . For a debut novelist, Akwaeke Emezi has successfully pulled off what many longtime writers only dream of doing. It's an astonishing, haunting, stunning piece of work." —Alex Brown, Tor.com

"Ambitious and original . . . Unconventional . . . Brilliant."

—Isabel Erickson White, *Zyzzyva*

"Emezi's tale of Ada's journey is astonishing."

—Jane Ciabattari, BBC

"Lyrical and dazzling . . . An intimate, spiritual, and haunting story; one that feels both unique and relatable in its exploration of identity . . . A stunning, genre-bending debut novel from a brilliant new writer—reading *Freshwater* is a transportive, otherworldly experience."
—Gina Mei, *Shondaland*

"In her mind-blowing debut, Emezi weaves traditional Igbo myth that turns the well-worn narrative of mental illness on its head, and in doing so she has ensured a place on the literary-fiction landscape as a writer to watch . . . Complex and dark, this novel will simultaneously challenge and reward lovers of literary fiction. A must-read."
—*Booklist* (starred review)

"[A] spiritually lush and tough yet lyrical debut . . . A gorgeous, unsettling look into the human psyche, richly conceived yet accessible to all."
—*Library Journal* (starred review)

"[An] enthralling, metaphysical debut novel . . . Emezi's talent is undeniable. She brilliantly depicts the conflict raging in the 'marble room' of Ada's psyche, resulting in an impressive debut."
—*Publishers Weekly*

"[A] haunting yet stunning exploration of mental illness grounded in traditional Nigerian spirituality . . . Employing precise and poetic yet accessible prose, Emezi brilliantly crafts distinct voices for each of Ada's selves and puts them in conversation with each other . . . She balances multiple lands, ethnicities, perspectives and belief systems with the ease of a writer far beyond her age and experience. *Freshwater* is a brutally beautiful rumination on consciousnesses and belief and a refreshing contribution to our literary landscape."
—*BookPage*

"Akwaeke Emezi is a major, exhilarating talent."

—NoViolet Bulawayo, Booker-shortlisted author of *We Need New Names*

"In Emezi's remarkable debut novel, *Freshwater*, we enter the lives of our protagonist, starting in Nigeria and ending in the United States. Every page is imbued with radiant prose, and a chorus of poetic voices. With a plot as alive and urgent as it is relatable, *Freshwater* is also solidly its own, brims with its unique preoccupations. Never before have I read a novel like it—one that speaks to the unification and separation of bodies and souls, the powers or lack thereof of gods and humans, and the long and arduous journey to claiming our many selves, or to setting our many selves free."

—Chinelo Okparanta, author of *Under the Udala Trees*

"With this stunning debut, Akwaeke Emezi has blessed us with nothing less than a masterpiece. *Freshwater* is a journey of loss and reconciliation, home and heartbreak, and ultimately a survivor's guide to harmonizing spirit and flesh. Quite simply a gorgeous, elegant, and brutal work of truthtelling. To repeat: A masterpiece." —Daniel José Older, *New York Times*–bestselling author of The Shadowshaper Cypher series

"Wow. The net effect is a feeling of being peeled open, and quickly finding that skinless place to be normal. More than any novel I can remember, it feels utterly present to the place we are in the world." —Binyavanga Wainaina, author of *One Day I Will Write About This Place*

FRESHWATER

FRESHWATER

AKWAEKE EMEZI

Grove Press
New York

Published simultaneously in Canada
Printed in the United States of America

First Grove Atlantic hardcover edition: February 2018
First Grove Atlantic paperback edition: December 2018

ISBN 978-0-8021-2899-7
eISBN 978-0-8021-6556-5

Library of Congress Cataloging-in-Publication data is available for this title.

Grove Press
an imprint of Grove Atlantic
154 West 14th Street
New York, NY 10011

Distributed by Publishers Group West

groveatlantic.com

21 10 9 8 7 6 5

For those of us
with one foot
on the other side.

FRESHWATER

Chapter One

I have lived many lives inside this body.
I lived many lives before they put me in this body.
I will live many lives when they take me out of it.

We

The first time our mother came for us, we screamed.

We were three and she was a snake, coiled up on the tile in the bathroom, waiting. But we had spent the last few years believing our body—thinking that our mother was someone different, a thin human with rouged cheekbones and large bottle-end glasses. And so we screamed. The demarcations are not that clear when you're new. There was a time before we had a body, when it was still building itself cell by cell inside the thin woman, meticulously producing organs, making systems. We used to flit in and out to see how the fetus was doing, whistling through the water it floated in and harmonizing with the songs the thin woman sang, Catholic hymns from her family, their bodies stored as ashes in the walls of a cathedral in Kuala Lumpur. It amused us to distort the chanting rhythm of the music, to twist it around the fetus till it kicked in glee. Sometimes we left the thin woman's body to float behind her and explore the house she kept, following her through the shell-blue walls, watching her as she pressed dough into rounds and chapatis bubbled under her hands.

She was small, with dark eyes and hair, light brown skin, and her name was Saachi. She'd been born sixth out of eight children, on the eleventh day of the sixth month, in Melaka, on the other side of the Indian Ocean. Later, she flew to London and married a man named Saul in a flurry of white sari, veil, and flowers. He was a forceful man with a rake's smile and deep brown skin, tight black coils cropped close to his head. He sang Jim Reeves in an exaggerated baritone, spoke fluent Russian and knew Latin, and danced the waltz. There were twelve years between them, but still, the couple was beautiful, well matched, moving through the gray city with grace.

By the time our body was embedded in her lining, they had moved to Nigeria and Saul was working for Queen Elizabeth Hospital in Umuahia. They already had a little boy, Chima, who had been born in Aba three years before, but for this baby (for us), it was important that they return to Umuahia, where Saul was born, and his father before him, and his before that. The blood following paths into the soil, oiling the gates, calling the prayer into flesh. Later, there would be another girl child, born back in Aba, and Saul would sing to both the girls in his baritone, teach them how to waltz, and look after their cats when they left him.

But before the girls were born, they (the thin woman and the forceful man) lived in a large house in the doctors' quarters, the place with the hibiscus outside and the shell blue inside. Saachi was a nurse, a practical woman, so between the both of them, the odds were good that the new baby would live. When we got tired of the house, we fluttered and swooped, playing in the compound and watching the yam tendrils crawl up their supporting sticks, the silk of corn drying up as it ripened, the swelling and patched yellowing of the mangoes before they fell. Saachi would sit and watch Saul fill two buckets with those mangoes and bring them to her. She ate them all the way from their skins through their wet flesh to her teeth scraping like dry bone against the seeds. Then she made mango jam, mango juice, mango everything. She ate ten to twenty of them each day, then a few of the large avocados, slicing those around the pit and scooping their butter down her throat. And so our fetus body was fed and we visited, and when we were tired of their world, we left for our own. Back then, we were still free. It was nothing to slip away, along the bitter streams of chalk.

In those Queen Elizabeth days, their taxi driver was a man who plastered the inside of his car with a slogan, NO SHORTCUT TO SUCCESS. The same words, growing thick as stickers piled on one another, some peeling and others glistening new. Every day, Saachi left her little boy, Chima, at home with his nanny, and the taxi driver would take her from the compound to Saul's clinic in the interior of the village. That morning (the day we died and were born), her labor started as they drove down the twisting red roads. The driver spun the wheel around, following her gasped orders, and took her to Aloma Hospital instead. As her body called to us and wrung itself out, all Saachi could focus on were those stickers, swarming around the seats, reminding her that the short way did not exist.

Meanwhile, we were wrenched, dragged through the gates, across a river, and through the back door of the thin woman's womb, thrust into the rippling water and the small sleeping body floating within. It was time. When the fetus had been housed, we were allowed freedom, but it was going to be alone, no longer flesh within a house but a house itself, and we were the one meant to live in it. We were used to the warm thuds of two heartbeats separated by walls of flesh and liquid, used to the option of leaving, of returning to the place we came from, free like spirits are meant to be. To be singled out and locked into the blurred consciousness of a little mind? We refused. It would be madness.

The thin woman's body was prone to quick labors. The boy, the first child, had been born in an hour, and a year after we were born, the third child would take only two. We, the middle, held the body against the pull for six. No shortcuts.

It was the sixth day of the sixth month.

Eventually, the doctors slid a needle into Saachi and fed her from a drip, fighting our resistance with drugs, expelling the body that was becoming ours. And so we were trapped by this unfamiliar birthing, this abomination of the fleshly, and this is how we ended up here.

* * *

We came from somewhere—everything does. When the transition is made from spirit to flesh, the gates are meant to be closed. It's a kindness. It would be cruel not to. Perhaps the gods forgot; they can be absentminded like that. Not maliciously—at least, not usually. But these are gods, after all, and they don't care about what happens to flesh, mostly because it is so slow and boring, unfamiliar and coarse. They don't pay much attention to it, except when it is collected, organized and souled.

By the time she (our body) struggled out into the world, slick and louder than a village of storms, the gates were left open. We should have been anchored in her by then, asleep inside her membranes and synched with her mind. That would have been the safest way. But since the gates were open, not closed against remembrance, we became confused. We were at once old and newborn. We were her and yet not. We were not conscious but we were alive—in fact, the main problem was that we were a distinct *we* instead of being fully and just *her*.

So there she was: a fat baby with thick, wet black hair. And there we were, infants in this world, blind and hungry, partly clinging to her flesh and the rest of us trailing behind in streams, through the open gates. We've always wanted to think that it was a careless thing the gods did, rather than a deliberate neglect. But what we think barely matters, even being who we are to them: their child. They are unknowable—anyone with sense realizes that—and they are about as gentle with their own children as they are with yours. Perhaps even less so, because your children are just weak bags of flesh with a timed soul. We, on the other hand—their children, the hatchlings, godlings, ọgbanje—can endure so much more horror. Not that this mattered—it was clear that she (the baby) was going to go mad.

We stayed asleep, but with our eyes open, still latched on to her body and her voice as she grew, in those first slow years when nothing and everything happens. She was moody, bright, a heaving sun. Violent. She screamed a lot. She was chubby and beautiful and insane if anyone had known enough to see it. They said she followed her father's side, the grandmother who was dead, for her dark skin and her thick hair. Saul did not name her after his mother, though, as perhaps another man would have. People were known to return in renovated bodies; it happens all the time. Nnamdi. Nnenna. But when he looked into the wet blackness of her eyes, he—surprisingly for a blind man, a modern man—did not make that mistake. Somehow, Saul knew that whatever looked back out of his child was not his mother, but someone, something else.

Everyone pressed into the air around her, pinching her cheeks and the fatty tissue layered underneath, pulled in by what they thought was her, when it was really us. Even asleep, there are things we cannot help, like pulling humans to us. They pull us too, but one at a time; we are selective like that. Saachi watched the visitors flock around the baby, concern sprouting in her like a green shoot. This was all new. Chima had been so quiet, so peaceful, cool to Saachi's heat. Disturbed, she looked for a pottu and found one, a dark circle of velvet black, a portable third eye, and she affixed it to the baby's forehead, on that smooth expanse of brand-new skin. A sun to repel the evil eye and thwart the intentions of wicked people who could coo at a child and then curse it under their breath. She was always a practical woman, Saachi. The odds were good that the child would live. At least the gods had chosen responsible humans, humans who loved her fiercely, since those first few years are when you are most likely to lose them. Still, it does not make up for what happened with the gates.

The human father, Saul, had missed the birth. We never paid him much attention when we were free—he was not interesting to us; he held no vessels or universes in his body. He was off buying crates of soft drinks for the guests while his wife fought us for different liberations. Saul was always that type of man, invested in status and image and social capital. Human things. But he allowed her name and it was later, when we were awake, that we knew that and understood at last why he'd been chosen. Many things start with a name.

After the boy Chima was born, Saul had asked for a daughter, so once our body arrived, he gave it a second name that meant "God answered." He meant gods answered. He meant that he called us and we answered. He didn't know what he meant. Humans often pray and forget what their mouths can do, forget that every ear is listening, that when you direct your longing to the gods, they can take that personally.

The church had refused to baptize the child without that second name; they considered her first name unchristian, pagan. At the christening, Saachi was still as thin and angular as London while Saul's stomach was curving out a little more than it used to, a settled swelling. He wore a white suit with wide lapels, a white tie lying on a black shirt, and he stood watching with his hands clasped as the priest marked the forehead of the baby cradled in his wife's arms. Saachi peered down through her thick glasses, focusing on the child with a calm seriousness, her white hat pressing on her long black hair, the maroon velvet of her dress severe at the shoulders. Chima stood next to his father in olive khaki, small, his head reaching only up to Saul's hands. The priest droned on and we slept in the child as the stale taste of blessed water soaked through her forehead and stretched into our realm. They kept calling a man's name, some christ, another god. The old water beckoned to him and, parallel to us, he turned his head.

The priest kept talking as the christ walked over, scattering borders, dragging a black ocean behind him. He ran his hands over the baby, pomegranate water and honey under his fingernails. She had fallen asleep as Saachi held her and she stirred a little under his touch, her eyelids fluttering. We turned over. He inclined his head, that foam of black curl, that nutshell skin, and stepped back. They had offered her to him and he would accept; he did not mind loving the child. Water trickled into her ear as the priest called her second name, the god's answer, the one the church had demanded because they didn't know the first name held more god than they could imagine.

Saul had consulted with his senior brother while picking out that first name. This brother, an uncle who died before we could remember him (a shame; if anyone might have known what to do about the gates, it would have been him), was named De Obinna and he was a teacher who had traveled into those interior villages and knew the things that were practiced there. They said he belonged to the Cherubim and Seraphim church, and it seems that he did, when he died. But he was also a man who knew the songs and dances of Uwummiri, the worship that is drowned in water. All water is connected. All freshwater comes out of the mouth of a python. When Saul had the sense not to name the child after her grandmother, De Obinna stepped in and suggested the first name, the one with all the god in it. Years later, Saul told the child that the name just meant "precious," but that translation is loose and inadequate, both correct and incomplete. The name meant, in its truest form, the egg of a python.

Before a christ-induced amnesia struck the humans, it was well known that the python was sacred, beyond reptile. It is the source of the stream, the flesh form of the god Ala, who is the earth herself, the judge and mother, the giver of law. On her lips man is born and there he spends his whole life. Ala holds the underworld replete in her womb, the dead flexing and flattening her belly, a crescent moon above her. It was taboo to kill her python, and of its egg, they would say, you cannot find it. And if you find it, they would add, you cannot touch it. For the egg of a python is the child of Ala, and the child of Ala is not, and can never be, intended for your hands.

This is the child Saul asked for, the prayer's flesh. It is better not to even say that her first name.

We called her the Ada.

So. The Ada belonged to us and Ala and Saachi, and as the child grew, there came a time when she would not move on all fours, as most babies do. She chose instead to wriggle, slithering on her stomach, pressing herself to the floor. Saachi watched her and wondered idly if she was too fat to crawl properly, observing her tight rolls of new flesh as they wormed across the carpet. "The child crawls like a serpent," she mentioned, on the phone to her own mother, across the Indian Ocean.

At the time, Saul ran a small clinic out of the boys' quarters of the apartment building they lived in on Ekenna Avenue, Number Seventeen, made out of thousands of small red bricks. The Ada got a tetanus injection at that clinic after her brother, Chima, handed their little sister a piece of wood with a nail stuck in it and said, "Hit her with this." We didn't think she would do it so we were not concerned, but he was the firstborn and she surprised us. We bled a lot and Saul gave us the injection himself, but the Ada has no scar so perhaps this memory is not real. We did not blame the little sister, for we were fond of her. Her name was Añuli. She was the last born, the amen at the end of a prayer, always a sweet child. There was a time when she used to speak in a language no one but us could understand, being fresh as she was from the other side (but whole, not like us), so we would chatter back to her in it and translate for our body's parents.

Early in the mornings, before Saul and Saachi were awake, the Ada (our body) used to sneak out of the apartment to visit the neighbors' children. They taught her how to steal powdered milk and clap it to the top of her mouth with her tongue, flaking it down in bits, that baby-smell sweetness. After a few years, Saul and Saachi moved the family down the street to Number Three, which had more bedrooms and an extra bathroom. Eventually Number Seventeen was demolished and someone built another building there, a house that looked nothing like the old one, with no red brick anywhere.

But the red bricks were still standing when Saachi potty trained our body, using a potty with a blue plastic seat. The Ada was perhaps three years old, half of six, something. She walked into the bathroom where the potty was and pulled down her panties, sitting carefully because she was good at this. She was good at other things too—crying, for example, which filled her with purpose, replenished all those little crevices of empty. So when she looked up and saw a large snake curled on the tile across from the potty, the first thing our body did was scream. The python raised its head and a length of its body, the rest coiled up, scales gliding gently over themselves. It did not blink. Through its eyes Ala looked at us, and through the Ada's eyes we looked at her—all of us looking upon each other for the first time.

We had a good scream: it was loud and used up most of our lungs. We paused only to drag in hot flurries of air for the next round. This screaming had been one of the first things Saachi noticed when our body was a baby. It became a running joke in the family: "Aiyoh, you have such a big mouth!"

Since Chima had been such a quiet child, no one had expected the Ada to be so loud. After Saachi fed Chima and bathed him, she could leave him in the playpen and he would just play, calmly, alone. When our body was six months old, Saachi took us to Malaysia, across the Indian Ocean, flying Pakistan Airlines with a layover in Karachi. The staff gave her a bassinet to put us in, but we cried with such force that Saachi slipped the Ada some chloral hydrate to make her shut up.

Back in Aba, Chima used to stare at us in awe because our body would scream any time we didn't get what we wanted. There are limitations in the flesh that intrinsically make no sense, constraints of this world that are diametrically opposed to the freedoms we had when we used to trail along those shell-blue walls and dip in and out of bodies at will. This world was meant to bend—that's how it had worked before our body slid through rings and walls of muscle, opened her eyes, filled her lungs with this world, and screamed our arrival. We stayed asleep, yet our presence shaped the Ada's body and her temperament. She pulled out all the buttons on the cushions and she drew on the walls. Everyone had gotten so used to the mischief and the screaming that when the Ada was staring at the snake, frozen in fear and projecting her terror through her mouth, they paid no attention. "She just wants her own way," they said, sitting around in the parlor, drinking bottles of Star beer. But this time, she didn't stop.

Saul frowned and exchanged a glance with his wife, concern flitting over their faces. He stood up and went to check on the child.

Now, Saul was a modern Igbo man. His medical training had been on scholarship in the Soviet Union, after which he spent many years in London. He did not believe in mumbo-jumbo, anything that would've said a snake could mean anything other than death. When he saw the Ada, his baby, with tears dripping down her face, blubbering in terror at a python, a wintered fear clutched at his heart. He snatched her up and away, took a machete, went back and hacked the python to bits. Ala (our mother) dissolved amid broken scales and pieces of flesh; she went back, she would not return. Saul was angry. It was an emotion that felt comfortable, like worn-in slippers. He strode back into the parlor, hand wrapped in bloody metal, and shouted at the rest of the house.

"When that child cries, don't take it for granted. Do you hear me?!" The Ada huddled in Saachi's arms, shaking.

He had no idea what he had done.

Chapter Two

The python will swallow anything whole.

We

This is all, ultimately, a litany of madness—the colors of it, the sounds it makes in heavy nights, the chirping of it across the shoulder of the morning. Think of brief insanities that are in you, not just the ones that blossomed as you grew into taller, more sinful versions of yourself, but the ones you were born with, tucked behind your liver. Take us, for instance.

We did not come alone. With a force like ours, we dragged other things along—a pact, bits of bone, an igneous rock, worn-out velveteen, a strip of human hide tying it all together. This compound object is called the iyi-ụwa, the oath of the world. It is a promise we made when we were free and floating, before we entered the Ada. The oath says that we will come back, that we will not stay in this world, that we are loyal to the other side.

When spirits like us are put inside flesh, this oath becomes a real object, one that functions as a bridge. It is usually buried or hidden because it is the way back, if you understand that the doorway is death. Humans who have sense always look for the iyi-ụwa, so they can dig it up or pull it from flesh, from wherever secret place it was kept, so they can destroy it, so their child's body will not die. If Ala's womb holds the underworld, then the iyi-ụwa is the shortcut back into it. If the Ada's human parents found it and destroyed it, we would never be able to go home.

We were not like other ọgbanje. We did not hide it under a tree or inside a river or in the tangled foundations of Saul's village house. No, we hid it better than that. We took it apart and we disseminated it. The Ada came with bones anyway—who would notice the odd fragments woven in? We hid the igneous rock in the pit of her stomach, between the mucus lining and the muscle layer. We knew it would weigh her down, but Ala carries a world of dead souls inside her—what is a simple stone to her child? We put the velveteen inside the walls of her vagina and we spat on the human hide, wetting like a stream. It rippled and came alive, then we stretched it from one of her shoulder blades to the other, draping it over her back and stitching it to her other skin. We made her the oath. To destroy it, they would have to destroy her. To keep her alive, they would have to send her back.

We made her ours in many ways, yet we were overwhelming to the child. Even though we lay curled and inactive inside her, she could already feel the unsettling our mere presence caused. We slept so poorly that first decade. The Ada kept having nightmares, terrifying dreams that drove her again and again into her parents' bed. It would be the inky hours of morning and she'd wake up in cold dripping fear, then tiptoe into their room, creaking the door open gently. Saul always slept on the side of the bed closest to the door with Saachi beside him, next to the window. The Ada would stand next to their bed with tears falling down her face, hugging her pillow until one of them sensed that she was there and woke up to find her silently sobbing in the dark, wearing her red pajamas with the white-striped top.

"What happened?" A thousand times.

"I had a bad dream."

Poor thing. It wasn't her fault—she didn't know that we lived in her, not yet. Like a child kicking in their sleep, we struck at her unknowing mind, tossing and turning her. The gates were open and she was the bridge. We had no control; we were always being pulled toward home, and when she was unconscious, there was more slip, more give in that direction.

The Ada surprised us, though, when she started to enter our realm. There would be a nightmare, ragged breaths of fear as we thrashed around, and then one night, she was suddenly there next to us, looking around at the dream, trying to get out. She was seven or eight and her eyes were young and calculating—she was brilliant, even before we sharpened her. That was one of the reasons Saul had married Saachi; he said he needed an intelligent woman to give him children who would be geniuses.

In the dream, the Ada imagined a spoon. It was strange, just a simple tablespoon, floating vertically. But it was metal and it was cold, and these things made it real. Next to it, all the bile we'd been creating was so obviously false. She looked at the spoon, identified which realm it belonged to (hers, not ours), and woke up. She did this over and over again, snapping out of the nightmares. Eventually, she didn't need the spoon at all. The dream would twist, getting dark, and the Ada would remind herself of where she was, that yes, she was in a dream filled with horror, but she still had the power to leave. With that, she'd drag herself out through glutinous layers of consciousness until she was awake, fully, rib seams aching. She, our little collection of flesh, had built a bridge all by herself. We were so proud. We watched her from our realm, in those times before we were ready to wake up.

And then, one day, awakening arrived.

It was December, during the harmattan, when the Ada was in the village. Saul always took the family to Umuecheọkụ for Christmas, and afterward, the Ada would go to Umuawa to spend the New Year with her best friend, Lisa. Lisa's family was a rowdy and boisterous clan, people who held the Ada in their arms and kissed her good night and good morning. The Ada wasn't used to so much contact. Saul and Saachi were not prone to holding, not like this. So she loved Lisa's family, and they were the ones who took her to the masquerade ceremony where our awakening arrived.

That night was black as velvet tamarind, thick in a way that made people walk closer to each other, pressing in a pack that moved down to the village square. The Ada could hear the music even before they reached the thudding crowd. One by one, people around her started tying bandannas and handkerchiefs over their noses and mouths before they plunged into the cloud of dust where everyone was dancing and throwing themselves to the music, to the sounds of the ekwe and the ogene.

Lisa handed her a white handkerchief, the cotton falling over her fingers like an egret's wing. The Ada paused at the edge, her sandals sinking briefly into the heavy pale sand, and she looked on. The quick beat of the ekwe went high and low, low low low, high high, the sound tight and loud. Lisa dipped into the crowd, her eyes crinkled with laughter above the red bandanna wrapping her face. The Ada felt her heart stagger with the ogene. She tied the handkerchief around her face and her feet lifted, throwing her into the dancing mass. The dust was weaving in the air, light against her face, softly scraping her eyes. It breathed on her skin. Sand flew up around her feet and the skin on her back prickled.

The drumming was shaking everything, and the crowd broke apart in mad rushes as the masquerades dashed at people, cracking whips and splitting the air. Their raffia flew wildly around them, the cowhide springing like a fountain from their hands. Their leashes were wrapped around their waists and their handlers shouted and pulled behind them as the masquerades flogged people with a sharp glee. The music sang commands in an old inherited language. It drifted into our sleep, our restless slumber; it called to us as clearly as blood.

Have you forgotten us already?

We fluttered. The voice was familiar, layered and many, metal tearing through the air. The ground pounded.

We have not forgotten any of your promises, nwanne anyị.

The air cracked as we remembered. It was the sound of our brothersisters, the other children of our mother, the ones who had not come across with us. Ndị otu. Ọgbanje. Their earthly masks whirled through the humans and they smelled like the gates, like sour chalk. Masquerade ceremonies invite spirits, giving them bodies and faces, and so they were here, recognizing us in the midst of their games.

What are you doing inside that small girl?

The Ada lifted up her arms and spun around. The people around her suddenly scattered and she ran with them, squealing as a masquerade lunged in their direction. It stopped and stood, swaying softly. It had a large face the color of old bone and a raw red mouth. It was draped in purple cloth and balancing a carved headdress, painted brightly. The moonlight poured over it. We trembled in our sleep, the taste of clean clay wiping through us. Our brothersister tilted its head and the headdress angled sharply against the black sky. It was irritated.

Wake up!

At the sound of its voice, deep within the Ada, deeper than the ash of her bones, our eyes tore open. The masquerade's handler tugged on the rope around its waist and it spun away. The Ada stood still for a moment before Lisa appeared, grabbing her hands and whirling her in a circle.

They all left a little after midnight, Lisa's cousins laughing and smashing beer bottles to the ground in a spray of green glass. Back at the house, the Ada untied the handkerchief and held it up, unfolded. There were three splotches of brown, two for her nostrils, one for her mouth. We wish she had saved it, but that is how humans are. Important things slip past in the moment, when it feels sharp and they are young enough to think that the feeling will remain. Later on, the Ada would remember that night with an unfamiliar clarity as one of the few genuinely happy times in her childhood. That moment, when our eyes opened in the dust of the village square and we were awake in both her realm and ours for the first time, it felt like pure brightness. We were all one, together, balanced for a brief velvet moment in a village night.

We've wondered in the years since then what she would have been without us, if she would have still gone mad. What if we had stayed asleep? What if she had remained locked in those years when she belonged to herself? Look at her, whirling around the compound wearing batik shorts and a cotton shirt, her long black hair braided into two arcs fastened with colored bands, her teeth gleaming and one slipper broken. Like a heaving sun.

The first madness was that we were born, that they stuffed a god into a bag of skin.

Chapter Three

What is a child who does not have a mother?

We

When we first entered this world, even after our eyes opened in the village, we remained fogged in newness. We were very young. But soon (a matter of years to you but nothing to us), we were forced into sharpness, forced by blood wiped along a tarred road, the separation of a bone at three points, and the migration of a mother.

Our brothersisters have always possessed the cruelty that is our birthright. They stacked their bitterness like a year's harvest; they bound it all together with anger, long memories, and petty ways. The Ada had not died, the oath had not been fulfilled, and we had not come home. They could not make us return because they were too far away, but they could do other things in the name of claiming our head. There is a method to this. First, harvest the heart and weaken the neck. Make the human mother leave. This, they knew, is how you break a child.

Saul and Saachi were living at Number Three then, with the children and Saul's niece Obiageli. Obiageli was one of De Obinna's two daughters, but she was not like her father, she did not know the right songs or dances or the source of the spring. She was Christian, decidedly so, blind in that way. But she loved the Ada, and sometimes, love is almost protection enough. When Obiageli's sister came to visit, Obiageli left her to babysit. Saachi had a rule: the children did not leave the house unless they were with her or Saul. She was a practical woman, so the odds were that the child would live.

Besides, the mischief of the Ada's infancy had progressed into moody troublemaking. She lost her temper frequently, slamming doors and fighting with Chima and Añuli, the increased weight of her body ricocheting off the walls of their house. Her anger would mutate hotly into bouts of uncontrolled weeping, until her lungs got tired. She was violent, and years later, it made even her human mother afraid. Saachi could not discipline the children in the ways that Saul and Obiageli could, not with fear, not like a Nigerian. But she did run a tight household; she was tough with anyone who didn't have her blood in them, and most of the time no one would have even dreamed of breaking her rules.

This cousin, however, was only visiting. The salt in the kitchen had finished and she needed to go to the shop to get some more, so she broke the rules and took the girls out of the house, because they begged to come with her on that hot and loud afternoon. It was meant to be a quick trip across Okigwe Road. All they had to do was turn left when they came out of the gate, walk past the man who sold sweets at Number Seven, turn left again at the red gate, and walk until they reached the main road.

The whole way, Añuli kept talking about crossing the road by herself; she'd seen other small children doing it and saw no reason she couldn't. They made it to the corner where the women sold roasted corn and yam and ube over hot coals, and they waited for a gap in the traffic. The Ada kept her hand inside her cousin's wrapped palm, but Añuli looked left, then broke free and darted, small, six, across the road. A pale blue pickup truck came in from the right and hit her with a sound like the world stopping.

The Ada screamed as Añuli fell onto the tarred darkness. The pickup couldn't stop. The driver tried but his brakes did not work, the truck could not stop, not even for her, not even for her small six-year-old self, for her Pink Panther T-shirt and shorts, the snagging of the cotton to its metal undercarriage, for the rubber slippers torn off her feet or the hooking of her shoulders and spine to the truck's skeleton. It dragged her small golden body away, down the road, smearing blood in burning tire trails. We (the Ada and us) do not remember our mouth's sounds, our own personal screams, nor those of the cousin. We do not remember how the road was crossed, who stood around, who reached out and unhooked the pink splattered cloth from the underside, what the pickup driver said, when Saul's neighbor arrived with the station wagon, who lifted Añuli's awake body from the road and put her in his backseat, or how many people were in the car.

We do remember how, in the car, our body twisted to look at Añuli screaming behind the driver's seat, her leg dug open from knee to ankle to bone, warm and red and gushing with shocks of white. The girls used to be mirrors, dressed alike, four horns curving down from the sides of two heads, before the truck tore one away from the other. The Ada was frantic, shouting, trying to think of how to fix it, who to handle it.

"Take her to our father's hospital, please," the Ada sobbed. The men in the car did not listen to her—the Ada was eight and she was wrong. They took Añuli to Lisa's father instead. He was an orthopedic surgeon, not a gynecologist like Saul. The electric signboard of his hospital was cracked from when someone threw a stone at it during one of the riots, and the building smelled like strong antiseptic and flesh that had gone off. Someone gave the Ada a Pepsi and took her next door to Lisa's house, while Lisa's mother sent their driver to fetch Saachi. When she arrived, the human mother entered the emergency room and looked at her youngest child, leg laid open on the examining table. Añuli's Pink Panther shirt had been cut open to get to her chest and it was stained dark with blood. Saachi cried and cried while our brothersisters smirked invisibly against the cabinets at the breaking they had begun.

Saul had been at the mechanic shop, and when he got to the hospital, Añuli asked him to give her an injection so that she could die. She had heard the doctors say they wanted to amputate her leg, and although she was small, she was already certain of what she could not live in this world without. Saul fought back tears as he reassured her, then he let them draw his blood for her transfusions. They took the Ada home, and for three days, she refused to visit her sister. Our brothersisters were pleased with that. Love for a human threatens the oath and makes spirits want to stay when they owe debts, when they should return.

Finally, Saachi sat down with the Ada. "Tell me," she said. "Why won't you go to the hospital?"

The Ada started sobbing. "It's my fault . . ."

Saachi looked at her, confused. "Ada, it's not your fault the car hit her."

"I'm the big sister . . . it's my j-job . . . t-to protect her . . ." She broke down wailing and Saachi put an arm around her, holding the child to her side and feeling the small shoulders curve in as they convulsed. We realized, later, that she was always a little uncertain when it came to her first daughter, what exactly to do with her, how to soothe such a force. It was understandable; it is always like this with ọgbanje, it is difficult for their mothers. If we could go back, we would tell Saachi what she realized only many years later: that none of the ways she tried to take care of this child would ever feel like enough.

"It's not your fault," Saachi repeated.

The Ada said nothing, but she didn't believe her. Duties were duties. We agreed with her on this. Over the years that followed, we (the Ada and us) became good at protecting Añuli, except for a terrible oversight in which we failed, for a very long time, to protect her from ourself.

At the hospital, they cast the amen's leg in plaster of Paris. They used a mechanical blade to cut the cast open every time they had to change it, then dressed the wound with sugar and honey. The first few times, they gave her narcotics to kill the pain, but then they had to stop, and she would scream and scream until the dressing was done. When it was over, she laughed. She was, to our surprise, not a being that the brothersisters could break so easily.

Saul's family came up from Umuahia to the hospital to see her, and old women in the ward drifted from the other beds to stand by Añuli's.

"Chai," they said dolefully. "What a beautiful child!"

"Ewo!"

"What a shame."

After about a week of this, Añuli turned to Saachi and asked if she was going to die. The human mother stared at her, this little girl who spoke of death so comfortably. We were not surprised, though. Had it not brushed past her on the bloody tar of that road? She was not afraid. Our brothersisters had touched her and she had lived. She asked Saachi that because she thought the visitors were there to mourn her approaching death, and we were impressed by this concept, to grieve the loss of breath while it was still in the body. After all, since we had been born to die, the Ada's life was a placeholder, an interlude; it made sense to start mourning it now.

The Ada became a precocious but easily bruised child, constantly pierced by the world, by words, by the taunts of Chima and his friends as they mocked her body for being soft and rounded. Reality was a difficult space for her to inhabit, unsurprisingly, what with one foot on the other side and gates in between. We wriggled deeply in her, reliving the blood of the backseat over and over again till the red was painted all inside. You must understand that Añuli's accident was a baptism in the best liquid, that mother of a color, then a clotting movement, a scrambled look at mortality and the weakness of the vessel. With our swollen new eyes, we saw the blood and knew it was a mantle.

We waited.

Things had not been easy for Saachi. They never are when you are the type of woman who gets chosen—just ask any other mother who has had a god grow inside her before spitting it out into a wild world. When Añuli was first born, Saachi became sick. The Ada was focused on her private mischiefs then—drawing on the walls and destroying the deep brown leather cushions by tugging on their threads. Chima was in school; he'd started Primary One down by Faulks Road. Saachi was drowning in anxiety. It rattled her chest and surged up her throat; it made her hands shake and then she cried and could not breathe. Saul did not help. He was an impatient man, a blind man. The children were always more Saachi's than his.

"I can't stay with you in the house!" he told his panicking wife. "I have work to do. If you have mental illness, then you'll just have to go to London."

That was it. Saachi had to turn to her friends, the women who had been born in other countries and who, like her, had accompanied their husbands to this small, violent town. Her friend Elena came by to check on her and Lisa's mother sent a girl in the evenings to stay with her, because Añuli was just a baby and Saul would not stay home and Saachi was drowning. Our brothersisters had known this, had known where the weak points in the Ada's family were, where to best apply pressure for a breaking. This was at Number Seventeen, at the red brick, and the next day, Saachi collected her three children and took them to Elena's house. She left them there and went to the hospital, where she stayed for two nights.

The doctors told her not to ingest any stimulants, and when they left her room, one of them, a woman, remained and asked Saachi kindly and quietly if everything was okay at home. Because it was strange, you see, the panic attacks and the way Saul was not there. Saachi said everything was fine. We do not know if she was lying, but the doctor prescribed medications to slow her heart rate, and after the second night, Saachi checked out, collected her children, and went back to Number Seventeen. She told herself that she would never be in that state again. Every day for a month, while the Ada and Chima played by themselves,

Saachi would put Añuli down on a woven mat, then lie on the sofa and cover herself with Chima's akwete blanket, all the way over her head, making a dark cave. The anxiety curled up on her chest like a cat and purred through her bones. She hid and hid, and Saul did not find her because he, as he had made clear, could not be at home with her and therefore was not looking.

It's like we said—things had not been easy for her. As she was drowning, the years slid past and the Ada's family moved down the street to Number Three. Then there was the truck and the amen and the impact and the blood. When Añuli could walk again, Saachi said that she would need plastic surgery, skin grafts for the river of glossy scar tissue running down toward her foot. She took Añuli back to Malaysia to consult with some doctors; she left the Ada behind. While on the trip, Saachi spoke to a nursing agent who offered her a job in Saudi Arabia.

There are many ways of breaking a family and isolating a child—our brothersisters knew this. Saul, for example, cared more about himself, so he was never going to protect the Ada and he was too human to be any kind of threat to the brothersisters. After career setbacks in London, he had been happy to end up in Nigeria, where he was hailed as a big man, coming from abroad with his Benz with the customized plates. He needed people to see him glow; he desired the glory of something. When Saul got his chieftaincy title, it was like he'd been dipped in silver, like he was finally as shiny as he wanted to be. He spent a lot of money on new things for himself, money that he refused to spend in other ways, like on his family. Saachi had to sew her traditional outfit for the ceremony out of an old sari. They'd fought over this and other things, like Saul refusing to buy things needed for the household. As his clinic struggled, Saachi kept transferring in money from her accounts in London. Immediately after the chieftaincy ceremony, instead of hosting the visitors who came to congratulate Saul, Saachi took the children to Onitsha to visit a friend and left a note for her husband.

"You may be a chief," she wrote, "but you are not a god."

She was correct, even more than she knew. He was not a god. He'd had to pray to one in order to get the Ada; she was not a child he could have created alone. Still, Saachi gave him many chances, windows and windows, ways he could have been worthy. In Malaysia with Añuli, after she got the job offer, Saachi called him.

"What do you think?" she said. "Should I take it? Will you be able to look after the children?"

"Let's talk about it when you get back," he said.

So she flew back to Nigeria with the amen, and by then, the Ada, who had never been without them for this long, almost didn't recognize them. We, however, knew already that forgetting could be protection.

Saul had paid for the trip, and when Saachi told him that the doctors had advised against skin grafts for Añuli's scar, recommending it be left as it was, Saul hissed. "So it was just a waste of my money, a wasted trip," he said, and then he walked away.

Saachi looked at his prideful back, then she looked at their bank accounts and at their family and she made a choice. It was easier to get free for the sake of her children than for the sake of herself—she did things for the Ada that Saul would never have lifted a finger to do. We admit, we accepted her because of that. She took the job and left the house at Number Three and as it turned out, she never lived there again.

Our brothersisters rejoiced from the other side—they had succeeded in chasing her away. No god would intervene, because ọgbanje are entitled to their vengeances; it is their nature, they are malicious spirits. Besides, there were many ways to look at what happened. Our brothersisters broke Saachi's heart, yes, but they also set her free, releasing her from the akwete blanket that Saul had condemned her to. If they had not thrown her last born into the road, she would never have gotten away. They meant to punish her: they took her children, they filled her mouth with sand. But it is only a fool who does not know that freedom is paid for in old clotted blood, in fresh reapings of it, in renewed scarifications. If Saachi did not know this before, then being a god's surrogate surely taught it to her. Such lessons are never easy.

The next five years of her life were contracted away in Saudi Arabia, and when that contract ended, Saachi called Saul.

"What do you think?" she asked. "Should I come back to Nigeria or should I try London?"

Saul had already left in all the ways that mattered, so it was not surprising that he said nothing, that his mouth was a gray space. Saachi was alone, and she knew that although Saul hated the money she made, he needed it. We thought he was weak; we knew he was chosen only because he would give the Ada her correct names. We did not pay attention to him.

In the face of his grayness, Saachi went to London, just to see what it was like and if, perhaps, she could move them all there. But when a depression seized her, she left and flew back to her deserts, to Saudi. By the time her last contract ended, the human mother had spent ten years there, from Riyadh to Jeddah and, finally, the mountains of Ta'if. She returned to Nigeria once or twice each year with suitcases that smelled cool and foreign. She left behind the sacrifice of three children fastened to an altar with thin sinews, and she would pay the costs of that for the rest of her life.

And this is how you break a child, you know. Step one, take the mother away.

Chapter Four

In the old culture, there would've been rites and rituals
for you to control the gates.
There were no rites or rituals done to help you control the gates.
You are the jewel at the heart of the lotus.

We

All the madnesses, each and every blinding one, they can all be traced back to the gates. Those carved monstrosities, those clay and chalk portals, existing everywhere and nowhere and all at once. They open, things are born, they close. The opening is easy, a pushing out, an expansion, an inhalation: the dust of divinity released into the world. It has to be a temporary channel, though, a thing that is sealed afterward, because the gates stink of knowledge, they cannot be left swinging wide like a slack mouth, leaking mindlessly. That would contaminate the human world—bodies are not meant to remember things from the other side. There are rules. But these are gods and they move like heated water, so the rules are softened and stretched. The gods do not care. It is not them, after all, that will pay the cost.

We were sent through carelessly, with a net of knowledge snarled around our ankles, not enough to tell us anything, just enough to trip us up. There are many neglects like this—little gods going mad around you, wandering the beaches with matted hair and swollen testicles. Unrecognizable, laughing through brown teeth as they grub through rubbish heaps, breasts stretched and groaning. That's what it looks like when the flesh doesn't take, when you can see them rejecting the graft of reality. But sometimes the flesh takes too well, like those that came through the gates and went mad in a much saner, more terrifying way, meeting human cruelty with colliding glee, losing themselves in the stringy red of mortality. They did atrocious and delicious things to torn people, to screaming and sobbing children: they broke and buried bodies, they hid in fathers and husbands, in mothers and cousins, they ripped and they used and they were excited. They took it too far. They took it only a god's length. For reasons like them, there should be a rule against shoving godspawn into a flesh-ridden cage. But they pull us, the humans, they draw us close. They're so turgid with potential and yet so empty, with spaces under their skins and inside their marrow, so much room for us to yawn into existence. They can be ridden, marked, anointed, fucked, then, sometimes, left.

Forgive us, we sound scattered. We were ejaculated into an unexpected limbo—too in-between, too god, too human, too halfway spirit bastard. Deity seed, you know. We never used to be alone, not in Ala's underworld womb, tucked in with the others, the brothersisters. Each time we left, we promised to come back, promised never to stay too long on the other side, promised to remember. We floated smoothly then, like a paste of palm oil, red and thick. Our mother was the world, even as she is now. But then she chose to answer some man's prayer and our smoothness was interrupted by the grain of his baritone. "Give me a daughter," he said. "Father Lord, give me a daughter."

Sometimes the only god who hears your prayer is the one who intends to answer it. We have never been able to understand why Ala answered this one, this particular request, in the crush of thousands of others; why she paid attention to this wrap of words. Perhaps the prayer caught her eye as it slid from Saul's mouth; perhaps she picked it on a whim, just to remind the world that she was still there, the owner of men. Since the corrupters broke her shrines and converted her children, how many of them were calling her name anymore?

We think about this because there has to be a point, a purpose to this, a reason for why we were thrust across the river, screeching and fighting. There must be a thought behind this entrapment, our having to endure this glut of humanity. On this, our mother, Ala, is silent. All we know is that there was a prayer, that the Ada was the answer, that our iyi-ụwa was hidden thoroughly in her body, making her the bridge between this world and ours. The rest is a road that spreads into unknowns. We were sentenced to those yawning gates between worlds, left wild, growing in all directions but closed. Open gates are like sores that can't stop grieving: they infect with space, gaps, widenings. Room where there should be none. We should have blended into the Ada when she was born, but instead there was a stretch of emptiness between us, bitter like kola, a sweep of nothing. A space like that has no place in a mind.

We used to be able to ignore it when we slept, but after we woke up in the village, our eyes opened and became swollen worlds with clouds for irises; the pupils, pots with no bottom. We could see everything. When Saachi left, we saw the way her children reeled, the way the Ada retreated deeper into her head, closer to us. She rooted like she'd lost her face, snuffling in the particular heartbreak of a little child, crying for her mother to come back, come back, please just come back. We struggled in response, coming alive not just for ourself, but for her. The Ada was so small, so sad. She should never have been left alone. She came looking for us because she was looking for anyone, because she was pursued by space, gray and malignant, cold as chalk.

She even tried to pray. They had been taking her to Mass every Sunday, telling her about the christ, the man who was a man and not. She read stories about how he would appear to his followers, the faithful ones, and so she prayed. She asked him to come down and hold her, just for a little bit. It would be easy for him because he was the christ and it would mean so much to her, so very much, just this little thing, because no one, you see, no one else was doing it, holding her. And besides, she loved him and she was a child, and even if she wasn't, he would love her anyway, but because she was, then it was extra because he loved the children most of all, so why wouldn't he just come down and hold one of them, just for a little bit?

We knew him; we knew his name was Yshwa, we knew that he looked like everyone, all at once, at any time. His face could shift like a ghost. It was, we also knew, impossible for him not to hear her. He hears every prayer babbled screamed sung at him. He does not, contrary to some belief, often answer them. Yshwa too was born with spread gates, born with a prophesying tongue and hands he brought over from the other side. And while he loves humans (he was born of one, lived and died as one), what they forget is that he loves them as a god does, which is to say, with a taste for suffering. So he watched the Ada cry herself to sleep with his wrong name and her mother's held on her lips. He ran his hands along the curve of her faith and felt its strength, that it would remain steadfast whether he came to her or not. And even if it did not hold, Yshwa had no intentions of manifesting. He had endured that abomination of the physical once and it was enough, never again. Not for the heartbroken children who were suffering more than her, not for the world off a cliff, not for a honey-soaked piece of bread. We resented him for it. When his fingers came too close, we snapped our teeth at them and Yshwa withdrew, amused, and went back to his watching.

We made ourself big and strong for the Ada, we tried to, because she was solidifying into something lost and bereft. We were still very weak, as newborns often are, but we were determined to spring into sentience, to drag ourself upright, clawing grips into the sides of her mind. We could not have done it if she was not the type of child that she was, ready to believe in anything.

Saul and Saachi had allowed the Ada to have a childhood that was, in a town full of death, unusually innocent. They didn't believe in interfering with the child's imagination, and so when the Ada finished one of her many books and decided that she could talk to animals, no one corrected her. "It did no harm to let her believe that," Saul said, and the Ada continued to believe wildly, in Yshwa and fairies and pixies living in the flame of the forest blossoms. She believed that the top of the plumeria tree in their backyard could be a portal to another world, and that all magic was stored outside in leaves and bark and grass and flowers. These things that she believed in meant that, although she did not know it yet, she could believe in us.

And so we were strengthened, because belief, for beings like us, is the colostrum of existence. After Saachi left, the Ada sank even more into her books, by instinct, separating herself from this world and disappearing into others. She read everywhere: on the toilet, at the dining table, in the library before school assembly each morning. It is not clear how much saving these books were capable of.

Meanwhile, Ala continued to watch her child. After all, the Ada was her hatchling, her bloodthirsty little sun, covered in translucent scales. We were learning that to be embodied was to be the altar and the flesh and the knife. Sometimes the gods just want to see what you are going to do.

Let us give you an example. When the Ada was seventeen, she was living in America, in a small town in the Appalachian Mountains. Saachi had moved her there for university and the Ada would have been alone, except that we were with her, we were always with her.

One night, we woke up with our body's heart racing, the air ricocheting with noise. It took us a moment to remember where we were, that we did not live in Aba anymore, that we were somewhere new. Our body was lying on a twin bed in a shared room, and a lean, dark, muscled boy was springing out of it, leaving us alone in his sheets. He answered the frantic knocking at the door and turned on the light, filling the room in yellow. His roommate looked over at our body, at the Ada, all the way from his bed against the other wall. He was the color of butter and his eyes were sour and hungry. There was an Eastern European girl at the door, one of the cross-country runners, tight spandex seized to her body. She had been splashed up and down with generous streaks of blood. Some of it was drying on her face, beside her dilated eyes, and she was telling the dark boy about another runner who had penetrated a window with his arm. The glass had penetrated him back, which explained her lavish coloring. The sour boy jumped down from his bed and we watched both of them pull shirts over their carved chests. The Ada slid down too, and we followed them out of the room and downstairs, our eyes tracing the drops of blood that were scattered down each step, then along the corridor. The runners kept talking and we slowed down until they had left us behind, then we turned and ran back up the stairs—drop drop drop, splatter on the wall—past the room we came out of, up the next staircase—drop drop, stain. On the second step, we found it—a puddle, a pool, a mirror, a small cloak. Deep like loss.

We looked around to make sure that we were alone, that no one was watching, but it was only the Ada and us and old banisters and worn carpet. We bent our knees and our breath was shallow, adrenaline coursing quickly; we reached out the Ada's hand until our fingertip brushed the surface of the pool, of the stale, exposed blood with its calm skin. It was already changing its mind about being liquid, cooling now that it was no longer merrily bouncing through the boy's blood vessels. We skimmed our fingers across the tight top of it, then the Ada stood up and we walked away, away from the terrifying rush of how much we wanted more of it, much more.

The problem with having gods like us wake up inside of you is that our hunger rises as well and someone, you see, has to feed us. Before the university, the Ada had begun the sacrifices that were necessary to keep us quiet, to stop us from driving her mad. She was only twelve then, and she sat at the back of her classroom and laid her hand on her desk, her palm flat. "Look," she said to her classmates, and they turned, vaguely interested. "Look what I can do." She raised the blade that she had taken from Saul's shaving supplies, that double-edged song wrapped in wax paper, and she dropped it on the skin of the back of her hand, in a stroke that whimpered. The skin sighed apart and there was a thin line of white before it blushed into furious red wetness.

She has no memory of her classmates' faces once that happened, because we filled her up utterly, expanding in glee, rewarding her for carving herself for us. She would spend another twelve years trying to be the torn feathers in a clay doorway, the sting of gin soaking the threshold. At sixteen, breaking a mirror to dig into her flesh with the glass. At twenty, when she was in veterinary school, after spending long hours separating skin from cadaver muscle and lifting delicate sheets of fascia, she would return to her room and use a fresh scalpel on her scarred left arm. Anything, you see, that would make that pale secret flesh sing that bright mother color.

Earlier, when we said she went mad, we lied. She has always been sane. It's just that she was contaminated with us, a godly parasite with many heads, roaring inside the marble room of her mind. Everyone knows the stories of hungry gods, ignored gods, bitter, scorned, and vengeful gods. First duty, feed your gods. If they live (like we do) inside your body, find a way, get creative, show them the red of your faith, of your flesh; quiet the voices with the lullaby of the altar. It's not as if you can escape us—where would you run to?

We had chosen the currency the Ada would pay us with back on the tar of Okigwe Road, in the maw of Añuli's leg, and she paid it quickly. Once there was blood, we subsided, temporarily sated. None of this had been easy for us, existing like this, entangled in two worlds. We did not mean to hurt the Ada, but we had made an oath and our brothersisters were pulling at us, shouting at us to come back. The gates were all wrong, everything was all wrong, we were not dying yet. But they kept pulling us, they made us scream, and we battered against the Ada's marble mind until she fed us and that thick red offering sounded almost like our mother—slowly, slowly, nwere nwayọ, take it slowly.

The Ada was just a child when these sacrifices began. She broke skin without fully knowing why; the intricacies of self-worship were lost on her. She did only what she had to and thought little of it. But she believed in us. Saachi brought back empty journals from Saudi Arabia and the Ada filled them up with blue ink. It was in them that she named us, titling us for the first time. Our forms were young and indistinct, but this naming was a second birth, it sorted us into something she could see. The first of us, Smoke, was a complicated gray, swirled layers and depths, barely held together in a vaguely human shape. We lifted our fogged arms, clumsy fingers exploring a blank and drifting face. The second of us, Shadow, was a deep black, pressed malevolently against a wall, hints of other colors (mother color eyes, yellowed teeth) that never made it past the fullness of the night. The Ada made us and continued to feed us.

Blood and belief. This is how the second madness began.

Chapter Five

Can you pray into your own ear?

We

After she named us in that second birth, we felt even closer to the Ada. This is not normal for beings like us; our brothersisters tend to have little or no affiliation to the bodies they pass through. The Ada should have been nothing more than a pawn, a construct of bone and blood and muscle, a weapon against her mother. But we had a loyalty to her, our little container. If we had been asked to take a piece of chalk and draw where she stops and where we start, it would have been hard. We did not know then how much of a betrayal this was to our brothersisters.

Our third birth happened in Virginia, after the Ada had moved to America. There was a song that followed us there, into the mountains, into the next split. It started in Sweden, and then it was flattened into a CD and bought in Germany, packed into the cool of a suitcase and carried into the humidity of Nigeria. Lisa unpacked it there and slid it into a CD player in her house in Aba, next door to her father's hospital where Añuli had been operated on. Lisa and the Ada listened to the song over and over again. The singer was a girl called Emilia and her voice went through the air of Lisa's room like a wing. When the Ada moved, she brought the song in a suitcase and she played it out loud in Virginia.

In another world, our third birth would have happened in Louisiana, among those swampy spirits, in the mouth of an alligator. There was a school there that gave the Ada a full scholarship, but Saachi diverted us from that path, swerving to avoid a cemetery, and she sent the Ada to Virginia instead. It was a smaller school, it would be quieter, and she thought the girl would be safer there. When she was making these choices, Saachi had tried to sit down with Saul in their dining room, under the painting of a grief-eyed christ, to plan the future of their children, which programs they would go to, which countries they would be lost to. But Saul had turned his back a long time ago—we could have told Saachi that.

"Why are you not interested in making college plans for them?" Saachi asked, hurt and frustration seeping out of the cracks in her voice. She wanted to include Saul; she was tired, ripped from her family, and she wanted him to care, to help. But Saul was an unforgiving man.

"What for?" he said. "I don't have the money." It was interesting for us to watch, how he didn't even have to go anywhere in order to leave her.

Saachi had been in Saudi for seven years by then—seven years of leaving her children, seven years alone. In all that time, Saul had never called her. Saachi would watch as the other women she worked with picked up their phones and broke into smiles at their husbands' voices, then she would leave quietly and cry to herself in her bedroom, before picking up the phone to call back home because she had not forgotten her children were still there, sacrificed and sad. She made their university plans alone, moving Chima to Malaysia to stay with her family there, then returning two years later to collect the Ada. They traveled to America together, stopping over in Addis Ababa. The Ada was excited because she knew Saachi always flew through Ethiopia—it was part of the human mother's other life, where she ate grapes reclining on embroidered cushions, acid-washed denim hidden under her abaya by yards of black cloth. When Saachi and the Ada flew through Addis, however, they spent only a few hours in the airport and it meant nothing, it felt like nothing. We were not surprised—many things are like this.

The Ada went to Virginia, to the slopes of grass and the marrow-red buildings of the school, heavy doors and creaking heaters throughout. It was winter when we arrived with Saachi and our body. There is a photograph of them, of Saachi and the Ada standing on a gentle incline with a church settled behind them and the ground suffocated in snow. Saachi's arms are lost in a black leather jacket and an oatmeal turtleneck wraps her neck like a large fist. Her hand is resting on the Ada's shoulder and they are both tightening their eyes against the sun. The Ada's legs stretch out from underneath an oversized fleece, dull mint green slinking over her wrists, and her hair is sticking out in tufts from under her woolen hat.

She is only sixteen, and the way she smiles, you can't tell we're in her, that we're puzzled by the snow and the cold and the damp roaring ocean between us and the red mud we came from, the drifts of white sand, that one palm tree that feels generations old, the one that wavers on the side of the road when you drive down from Ubakala Junction, before you pass all the seven villages, like sliding down the gullet of our mother, past the screaming gates of her teeth. It's not the first time we've been away, but it's the first time we don't know when we're coming back. We had no idea then that the song had followed us.

It was later, years later, when everything had changed, or before or right around, that the Ada lay in a narrow dorm bed in Hodges Hall next to a boy from Denmark and they both looked up at the ceiling. It was springtime and the room was quiet as the boy sang Emilia's song into the silence, the first two lines of the chorus. *I'm a big big girl in a big big world.* The Ada didn't pause, not a beat, and she sang the next two lines softly. *It's not a big big thing if you leeeaave me.* The boy sat up on his elbow, pleasantly surprised that she knew the song, asking her how, when, where. The Ada smiled at his delight and told him about Lisa's house and the pop CD from Germany, and yes, now we recall, this was before it all went rotten. It was only later, much later, that we discovered the staggering breadth of things this boy would do to the Ada.

* * *

The first few weeks of America were cold and the snow fell thickly, like it was being shoveled out of the sky. It was the Ada's first winter and she made a snow angel because that's what she'd waited for, to lie with her arms flung and her legs wide, to flap and fly until sainthood spread beneath her. Saachi stayed for two weeks before she flew to see Chima, before returning to Saudi, again with a stopover in Addis, leaving the Ada more alone than she had ever been.

We felt just like she did, the most alone we could remember, torn from the place of our first and second births: taken on a plane across an ocean, given no return date. Let us tell you, our mother's children began to cherish another great anger against us then. This was a side effect of being in a body, the fact that the humans had a human life. It was inevitable that the Ada would go to university, that her life would continue moving in a way that had nothing to do with us. She was majoring in biology; she wanted to be a veterinarian because she loved animals. We did not care. We were hungry inside her, raging against this useless mortality, as if we could rage right back to the world we came from. We raged at the displacement of a new country.

After all, were we not ọgbanje? It was an insult to be subject to the decisions made around what was just a vessel. To be carried away like cargo, to be deposited in the land of the corrupters, inside this child simmering with emotions, searching for us because she was uprooted and alone, and we, always we, having to fix it, well, you miss your father—why we don't know, the man was just a man, and you miss the amen and that yellow girl you used to run around with, and you have work to do, work to do, and no time to shatter any further, and you hide in a lecture hall and cry and cry as if you have something to cry about? Very well, we will do you this one thing, because it was always you and us together, and you named us the shadow that eats things and the smoke that hides the mother color from our teeth, and you have granted us dominion over this marble room that you call your mind, so here is the place where you miss that man and the girls and the road you used to run down, it is soft and fleshy, a bulb of feeling, and here we are like a useful edge and here is the cut, here is the fall, here is the empty that follows it all.

Here is the empty that follows it all.

After that, it was simple; the Ada stopped missing Saul and the amen and Lisa. We were still angry; gods are not appeased that easily, so we bubbled violently through her arms. She threw lamps and cafeteria cups across the small room she shared with a white girl on the honors floor, shattered glass following her like a lost dog. She met the American girls who had come from Miami and Atlanta and Chicago, Black girls with slick, straight hair. They fluttered at the state of hers, which was a confused mix of textures and lengths, thick and awkward. When the Ada was a child, it had been a beast leaping from her scalp and gnawing at her small shoulders. Saachi bought relaxers to subdue it, to stop it from rising into the sky; not to make it straight but to calm it down so at least a comb could be teased through. It was washed every Sunday in its full greatness, combed through every morning before school, tugged into two plaits while the Ada ate Nasco cornflakes and winced.

Saachi was in Saudi the day that they cut it, but she spoke of that day as if she was there, telling everyone how the Ada cried. In the months before leaving for America, the Ada had let her hair grow back out, braided it into synthetic twists for her secondary school graduation, then taken those out before flying to Virginia. The American girls sat her down firmly in front of a television and relaxed her hair, blow-drying and flat-ironing it until it was decided and bone-straight. The girl holding the flatiron sang along to the advertisements on TV and the Ada laughed, looking up at her sideways.

"How do you know all the songs?" she asked.

The girl laughed back at her. "Don't worry," she said. "By the time you're here for a while, you'll be singing all the commercials too." She ran a wide-tooth comb through the Ada's hair, admiring how all the curls had gone. The other girls came to check it out, to give their approval, and then they took her around to meet the other Black kids on campus, because the Ada was now one of them, welcome to America. We watched, fascinated. Humans are so ritualistic. When they met her, the Black boys sidled up, grinning. Most of them were track runners, tight and almost feline in how they moved.

"Hey girl," they drawled. "Where you from?"

It wasn't a question we were used to, not yet. "Nigeria," the Ada replied, smiling politely, wondering if it sounded strange. We never had to say that when we lived there.

"Oh, word? That's cool."

The girls who were showing her around leaned against the walls and flipped their silked-up hair. "Watch out now," they said, smirking. "She's only sixteen."

The Ada watched as the boys visibly recoiled.

"Oh, hell no!" they said, drawing out the hell. "We gon' have to wait till you eighteen, shit."

Everyone laughed and the Ada smiled vaguely, but she didn't get the joke, not then. After a few weeks with that crew, it became clear that the Ada didn't quite fit. They disliked the white equestrians who lived on the honors floor with her, and the Ada didn't know why, not yet. America would teach her that later. When the Black kids found out that she listened to Linkin Park, they looked at her like she was a stranger thing than they'd bargained for. The Ada drifted away from them and found the other international students instead: the long jumper from Jamaica, the soccer players from Saint Lucia and Uganda and Kenya, the Dominican cigar-smoking girl, all the others who didn't quite fit either. They became her circle for the rest of her stay in the mountains.

Then it was two years later and she was eighteen and her hair was long and decided and bone-straight, falling past her shoulders in heavy dark brown. We were still inside her, but she was much the same as she'd been when Saachi brought her there and handed her over to the kindly white faculty, except she now knew what everyone meant by the jokes about her age, she knew what they were waiting for. The Ada still wore a gold crucifix around her neck, a gift from Saachi's mother, a reminder that she had kept her childhood crush on the christ. She never questioned his decision not to hold her; instead she constantly asked him for forgiveness as she tried to be worthy of his love. There had been the Panamanian boy when she was sixteen (sixteen and a half, she'd corrected, and he looked at her like she was a child), the dark muscled boy from Canarsie who ate no meat and taught her how to twist his dreadlocks and braid them, the assistant track coach from Colombia, the embarrassing crushes (the man from admissions, the skinny Trini boy who ran like wind on the pitch)—all just kisses, no one had touched her lower than the indent of her navel.

We kept her neutral. It was strange; it had been strange even when we were home (back across the ocean, where we belonged). There was one day when Lisa had come out from her boyfriend's room and told the Ada about the splash of white that colored his trousers from the inside, and our body just arranged her face the way it was supposed to look, as if she understood the secrets of hot teenage fumblings or the appeal of shiny condoms. She knew, logically, but we kept her neutral. It was not meant for her, the heat rising, the tricks of the body, the compulsions of flesh. She turned eighteen and nothing happened. We kept her. They watched her move in her innocence, a golden chained thing, dancing on dim dance floors and bright stages, winding circles with her waist as if she'd done so on a body before. She tried to hide it, flirting and kissing as if she had fire inside rather than us. All those boys, all that empty following it all. We kept her, we held her, she was ours.

There was a Serbian boy with clear brown eyes who was different, who mattered to the Ada very much. His name was Luka and he was on the tennis team. He lived in the house down the hill and had dark hair, even on the gap of his chest that showed through his shirts and on his forearms and calves. Luka knew the Ada enough to see when the blood rose to a blush through her brown skin and he had been a safe place, a port, a boy who called the Ada magic and wanted more than the friendship she offered. He stopped when she chose someone else, later, afterward, when she had no safe places outside her anymore.

The Ada used to go to Luka's house down the hill, where their friends drank to prepare for the night out, rolling joints and snorting quick lines of coke. The house was full of volleyball players, tall Europeans who were sweet, affectionate, open.

"Come to Iceland," Axel said, his blond hair falling over his beautiful cheekbones, bending down to forgive his height. "Come and see the northern lights, they're wonderful."

A year later, he would climb up a fire escape, rumpled and handsome in a linen suit, to kiss her, and she would be sad because he was so carelessly lovely but everything was too late. But then, back then, he was bright and drunk and high, and he and his best friend, the Slovakian, Denis, played Pac-Man with mad concentration. Together with Luka, they were that house that drew everyone in, the center. She liked them, she liked being around them, because when she came over, they already knew she didn't drink or smoke, and so they played music she liked instead, with horns blasting, and we would dance inside her like those days when we used to dance with Saachi before she birthed our cage. We danced through her body, our body, the one that had been built so carefully for us, now winding through the rooms, her hands swirling in the air, the music repeating as the boys played it for as long as she wanted, the only fix they could offer, the only one she'd take.

We were distinct in her head by then: we had been Smoke and Shadow since the naming, since the second birth, little nagging parts that the Ada tried to ignore, that she sometimes argued with but didn't tell anyone about. She just went down the hill, danced until her long hair smelled of smoke or until everyone left for Gilligan's, where she'd been going before she was legal because the club took college IDs as if they were real, as if everyone started college at eighteen. It was at the house down the hill that she met the boy who would sing the Emilia song a few months afterward. His name was Soren. He was one of the volleyball players, Danish according to his passport, Eritrean according to his blood, a skinny boy with pools for eyes and dark spilling smooth on his skin. We noticed him. He noticed the Ada because she didn't drink, didn't smoke, only danced, and there was something in her, something he wanted to put his fingers on. He walked beside her as they all left the house in a rowdy crowd.

"Do you smoke?" he asked, to be sure.

She thought he meant cigarettes. So did we. "No," she answered.

He'd meant weed, but he liked her answer. They danced together in the smoke of Gilligan's that night, slowly. The club was named after a TV show that she'd never seen, very plastic and Hawaiian, with fake parrots and violently colorful drinks. The first time the Ada went there, she'd stared in shock at the way people ground against each other, ass to crotch, lost in smoke; she'd stared at the dangerous fall of jeans lower than hips, at the bad behavior of it all. They always played "Sandstorm" and, later, at the end of the night, "New York, New York" as a kind of dramatic finale. By her last semester, the Ada would be up on that stage, arms around a line of strange white girls, kicking her legs up to Frank Sinatra's hymn to Manhattan and dreaming of the day she'd live there.

But that night, beer was slippery under their feet as Soren touched his lips to the angles of her hand and the curve of her neck. He had the fullest eyes she had ever seen, so she let him come back to her dorm room with her. The Ada lived alone then, as a resident assistant, so she could smash mirrors and make carpets of fine glass in peace and quiet. She could feed us with cuts without having to explain or having people think something was wrong with her. That night, she brought him into her room and they kissed and fell asleep. Soren returned every day after that.

He cried a lot, that boy, with those doe-dark eyes of his. The Ada pretended not to hear, but we listened intently as he huddled against the white brick wall and sobbed into the night, dreams driving him away from sleep. In the day, he couldn't stand to be apart from her for too long. He held her constantly (we liked that). One day, when they were getting breakfast in the cafeteria, the Ada filled her plate with six hard-boiled eggs and brought them to the table.

"Don't eat that," Soren said. "It's too many eggs."

She stared at him and laughed, then started cracking the eggs against each other, point to point, like gladiators. Whichever broke first got eaten. The winner survived till the next round.

Soren stared at her, his face blank. "I said, you can't eat that." He didn't raise his voice.

The Ada frowned at him and ate her eggs, curious about the harm she could smell in his gentleness, surprised that he thought he could command her. He said nothing more and ate his breakfast, his smooth face moody, his slim shoulders curved over his plate. The next day, he called her his girlfriend.

"Wait, really?" she replied. "I didn't know that." Her answer made him angry, which irritated her.

"How can you not know that? What do you think we've been doing?" he asked.

"How am I supposed to know if you're just now telling me?" the Ada replied, but Soren stayed angry.

That was the first thing that made us interested in him—his anger. His rich, thick blood sap anger. His nightmare childhood trauma anger. His I was taken when I was little and the men kept me in a dirty, small room and they never found the other child anger. You could taste the sharp sting of it, the salty frantic colors it had. He was angry that the Ada didn't know she was his girlfriend; he was angry because she performed indifference, telling him he could end it if he wanted to, he could leave if he wanted to. He was angry when she suggested he wasn't over his ex-girlfriend, angry when she tried to walk out of their arguments, angry when she ran and hid in a basement to get away from him.

We were fascinated by the ease with which he slipped into his rages, how much he looked like a little boy when he stormed off down the hallway, his slippers thick and plastic and slapping against the carpeting. None of it really touched us. The Ada was performing other things, acting the role of a normal girl in college, selling kisses in order to be held. She had many conversations with her christ, always one-sided, trying to decipher what he wanted. The abstinence was easy for her; she had always been interested in sex only from odd, indirect angles, reading the Bible for perversions, trying to learn all the words, all the pieces of it that only fit in the mind. Her body, our body, was indifferent. When the other girls talked about their lusts, she listened curiously to these hungers she didn't have, a need neither she nor we understood. When Soren tried to fuck her, she did not understand. We didn't understand either. We were only interested in his pain.

He was full of shame and apologies when she said no. The Ada smiled and explained her vow to the christ, explained how important it was to her while fingering the gold crucifix around her neck. Her grandmother on Saachi's side would have been proud. After that, the Ada watched with a mild interest when Soren slid his penis between her breasts. She found herself still watching as she moved into his dorm room for the May term, still watching when he raged about his father, when he punched the walls till his hands swelled. We watched with her, observing this furious human and his hungers. One evening, Soren stood up from the bed and looked down at our body.

"You need to get birth control pills." His voice was calm, a pool of quietly congealing blood with a skin forming.

The Ada didn't understand. She blinked and there was a pause, a teetering moment. She had no idea what he was talking about. Then slowly, information started filtering through, edged with alarm. Plain details at first, like it was afternoon and the trees outside the window were green in the sunlight. Like he was naked but she had no idea what she was wearing. Like his penis was out and it was brown like his eyes. Like how she didn't remember taking anything off or putting anything on. He pulled on a pair of shorts as she sat in the cheap Wal-Mart sheets, knowledge trickling like warm urine into her head, traveling down to her chilled hands. The words swirled in nausea around her. Birth control pills, because this boy, this boy with the doe eyes and the sad skin, had released clouds into her. But she couldn't remember any of it and she couldn't remember saying yes because she couldn't remember being asked.

She was confused. There had been so many refusals in the weeks before, piled up like small red bricks, the weight of an apartment building that got torn down, things she thought would be heavy enough to hold him away because he knew, he knew, he knew she didn't want to. She couldn't remember anything, like was this the first time, was it the fifth, oh god, how long had he been moving unwanted parts of himself in her? The rush of unknowns propelled the Ada out of the bed and she slid her feet into sneakers and laced them up as fast as she could. Her burst of motion alarmed Soren; he hated when she left, so he grabbed her arms, forcing her to stay, shouting words, more words than she could listen to. She moved blindly against him, thinking only of the door, of away. He wanted her to say something, so he kept shouting. The Ada opened her mouth and all that poured out were large shapes of pain that flooded the air as her legs gave out. She crumpled to the floor and he dropped down with her. They sat together in shambled sheets as he shouted blank words at her.

She started to scream. She screamed and screamed and screamed. Her vision was numb. There was a window in front of her but it opened into a nothingness like the one yawning from her mouth. Somewhere she could hear a building sound, a wind, huge and wide, rushing out of the void, rushing toward her. The walls, the veils in her head, they tore, they ripped, they collapsed. The wind rushed over his empty voice and the Ada thought with a sudden final clarity—

She has come. She has come for me at last.

ASỤGHARA

Chapter Six

Ọbịara egbum, gbuo onwe ya.

Asụghara

Of course I came. Why wouldn't I? Let me tell you, Ada meant every world to me. But I can't lie; this third birth of a thing was a shock. I had been there, just minding my own business as part of a shifting cloud, then the next thing I knew, I was condensing into the marble room of Ada's mind, with time moving slower for me than for her. The first thing I did was step forward so I could see through her eyes. There was a window in front of her face and one useless boy beside her. It was cold. I looked around the marble for Ada and there she was, a shred in the corner, a gibbering baby. I didn't touch her—that wasn't my style. I've never been the comforting type. Instead I sank my roots into her body, finding my grip on her capillaries and organs. I already knew that Ada was mine: mine to move and take and save. I stood her body up. The boy was crying and angry, still sitting on the floor.

"Go then!" he said, sulking. "Go!"

I made Ada pick up his jacket, and then she and I walked outside. Once we were away from him, I released her and focused on the rush of being here. I felt drunk and full of life; it flooded the pockets of my cheeks. I was a me! I had a self! I spun in the marble, giddy and ecstatic at existence, before remembering the reason I'd arrived. I swung around to check on Ada.

She was stumbling in front of Hodges Hall, dialing the phone number of one of her friends, an older Nigerian girl called Itohan, who lived in Georgia. I listened because honestly, it was just fascinating to have ears, to hear how Ada's voice reverberated inside her skull. She was sobbing as she told Itohan what happened, or at least what she could remember of what happened. I didn't interfere until Itohan told Ada to pray, that their God would forgive her. That didn't even make sense to me. Forgive her for what? I slid in gently and made Ada end the call. I could already see that she was clearly better off with just me.

Ada ran her arms through the bushes under the boy's window and the thorns scratched her skin bloody. She wept. I didn't mind the bleeding; it made me feel good, just like it always had, back when I was only a drift in the shifting cloud of the rest of us, floating through her. She walked across the road, over a small green hill, where there was a church and a graveyard. In the center of the graveyard, there was a cross that was seven feet tall. Ada wrapped her bleeding arms in the boy's jacket and lay on the concrete base, staring up into the sky as she cried some more. I lay down there with her, stretching through her. I wondered if she could feel that she wasn't alone. Her thoughts were translucent streams fogging up the marble—how she had disappointed her christ, how she wouldn't be able to pray again, not now, not ever. She knew what she was supposed to do—forgive herself for fucking and talk to the christ—except that she couldn't do either and she didn't think it mattered; she didn't think she was worth forgiving anyway. I watched her thoughts and frowned. She seemed very lonely. Poor thing, I thought, to be so in love with this christ. Why disturb herself with him if it was giving her so much pain?

But I liked her other choices, like the graveyard and the drying blood on her arms. Ada stayed there until the sun set, then I moved her to the house down the hill. She seemed to have good memories of that place and her friend there, Luka. He had left for the summer so his room was empty. It still smelled like him, though, and it felt like a safe place for Ada, so she hid in it. But the boy, Soren, he came looking for her there. It was something I was going to have to teach her, that there were no safe places left.

He was angry that Ada had disappeared and furious when he saw the crusted scratches on her forearms. He took her back to his room, and the wounds on her arms didn't stop him, the memory of her sitting in the sheets and screaming didn't stop him. No, the boy fucked her body again, that day and every day afterward, over and over. He would look into her eyes and swear in time with his thrusts as he fucked her, never bothering with a condom, always coming inside her.

"I fucking love you. You have no idea how much I fucking love you."

Except Ada wasn't there anymore. At all, at all. She wasn't even a small thing curled up in the corner of her marble. There was only me. I expanded against the walls, filling it up and blocking her out completely. She was gone. She might as well have been dead. I was powerful and I was mad, he could not touch me no matter how hard he pushed into her body, he could definitely never touch her. I was here. I was everything. I was everywhere. And so I smiled at him, using only Ada's mouth and teeth.

"You love this," I corrected. "You love fucking me."

He got angry again. The boy was so predictable, so easy to provoke. Human beings are useless like that. I liked making him angry, sha. I would hold him with Ada's arms and smile in the dark while he cried after his nightmares. It was good that he lived with pain. Ada was never there when there was a bed. If I made sure of anything in my short life till then, I made sure of that.

When she had to go and get a pregnancy test, the first of many, Ada called a taxi from the clinic and took it back to campus. The driver was a biker. She could tell because he had Harley-Davidson stickers everywhere. They reminded me of the other taxi, the one Ada's mother took in another lifetime, when we were both born. I was fond of stickers in taxis, so I said, with Ada's mouth, "I love motorcycles."

"You should give me a call," the driver replied. "I'll take you out on my bike one day." He gave Ada his card. The boy lost his temper when he found out and ripped the card into pieces. A few days later, he found Ada out back behind the dorm, weighing a broadsword with both hands, looking at knives that one of her collector friends had brought over in his truck. The boy got angry and banned Ada from ever playing with blades again. Ada looked at him and I stared through her eyes and kept her silent. She and I watched his anger bounce around and we did nothing, said nothing. What was there to say? It was more interesting to watch his fury grow at the dullness in Ada's eyes, the smooth emptiness of her face. It is not easy to look at me, I know this very well.

When Ada first met the boy, he told her this story about how much he loved his mother, how he and his brother went and drove nails through the hands of a man who threw stones at her in Denmark. I remembered it when I arrived. The image of the man being held against the ground, his palm forced open, the boys baring their teeth. The nail tearing through flesh and ligaments with metal purpose, the man's screams, the blood bursting. It was true, and me, I like true things. Yet, when Ada started to think that she loved the boy, I allowed it. It would make things easier for her. She was not like me; she was not strong. One time, the boy was leaving for a volleyball tournament and Ada held her hand to his face as they said good-bye. I watched through her eyes as his smile went away.

"Stop it," he told her. "My mother looks at me like that."

She must have been in front of me that time. I never looked at him with anything that could have been contained in his mother's face. The boy made Ada a gibbering thing in a corner—this is the truth, but he would never get her again. I had arrived, flesh from flesh, true blood from true blood. I was the wildness under the skin, the skin into a weapon, the weapon over the flesh. I was here. No one would ever touch her again.

When the May term ended, Ada left her school and that little run-down town in the pretty mountains, and flew to Georgia to stay with Itohan. Soren flew to Denmark, but he took her teddy bear, Hershey, with him. If you didn't know him, you could call that cute, but he was such a thief, you know, he stole and stole and stole. Fucking bastard. In Georgia, Itohan took Ada to a hair salon. Ada sat in one of the raised chairs and stared at her reflection, all that heavy hair hanging from her scalp.

"Cut it off," she said.

The stylists, even the other clients, were appalled. They were Black women who paid and took money to get and give long hair, thick hair, straight hair, and she had it pouring from her head like an afterthought.

"All that pretty hair?" they asked, horrified. "You sure?"

"I'm sure," Ada said. Of course she was sure. I was sure. Me, I remembered when Ada had been born, with wet hair that was black as jet and slick as a fish. The hair she had now was dead, deader than hair usually is. Besides, I had arrived and something had to mark that, so cutting her hair felt correct.

"Make the first cut then," the stylist said. She didn't believe Ada would do it, but she didn't know her and she certainly didn't know us.

Ada took the scissors from her, took a piece of hair from right above her forehead, pulled it down before her eyes, and snipped near the roots. The women in the room gasped, staring in shock. I grinned—shebi I told you the girl belonged to me now. Ada dropped the hair into her lap, on the smock they had put around her neck.

"Can you cut the rest, please?" she said.

The stylist shook her head and took the scissors from her. When she finished, Ada asked for her eyebrows to be waxed, and then she walked out of the salon, looking more like me. She was about to turn nineteen. Back at Itohan's apartment, she called another boy in Virginia, the brother of a friend, who'd arrived from Togo the semester before with a starched wide shirt collar that made Ada think of home. He and Ada had been flirting for hours each day, ever since the summer started. There were a few days when he wouldn't take her calls, after she told him about Soren, that she had a boyfriend. I grimaced when she said that, but I had promised to let her hold her lies if they would keep her sane. After a while, the brother called her and said it didn't matter. Somehow, that made it easier. Ada called Soren and told him she was breaking up with him. I stood heavy in her bones when she did it. The boy was so boring in his sobbing anger, I had her hang up on him. Ada never got her teddy bear back. I told you he was a thief.

After Georgia, Ada went to see Saachi, who was softer in the body now. The human mother had moved to America the year before. She stopped in Nigeria first to collect Añuli, then they went to America and rented a small apartment in a town in the Southwest. Saachi had wanted Saul to come because he could get his green card, but old failures in London meant he wouldn't be able to practice medicine in America, so the man refused.

"What am I going there to do? To go and sell popcorn?" he said.

"And what's wrong with that?" Saachi had replied. She didn't believe in pride when it came to Ada and the others. But Saul was the way he had always been, so Saachi and Añuli moved without him. The two of them lived in the one-bedroom space and Añuli slept on a futon in a small room with no door, next to the kitchenette. When Ada came to visit, she slept on the sofa in the living room. One morning, she woke up and Saachi was standing in the kitchenette, looking at her. She was holding a cup of coffee and Ada knew it would be black, just like she knew all of Saachi's glasses of Coke would be laced with Bacardi. Many things were always the same.

"When you sleep," Saachi said, as if it was nothing, "you look exactly how you did as a child. Exactly."

Ada rubbed her eyes, and when she opened them again, Saachi had walked out of the room and she was alone. They had argued about Ada's haircut when she first got there, and Saachi had left Bible verses in the bathroom on Post-it notes, about how a woman's hair was her crown. I had Ada ignore the notes. She was still getting used to moving with me; I was heavy and I made her different, or maybe he had made her different, but either way, nothing was the same. Saachi watched her like she always had, ever since Ada was a fat baby with a protective pottu on her forehead.

"You used to smile," Saachi said. "You were such a happy child. Why are you not eating?"

This was actually true, but the not eating was just an experiment I was doing, to see how close to the bone I could get Ada down to. She had started restricting by herself before I showed up, for some human reason, probably trying to control her body since she couldn't control her mind. It's not important. The point is once I was there, I took her to new weightless places. 118 pounds. She ran every day for an hour. I had her eat only salads. Hunger grabbed her from the inside, intimately. It felt like it had a purpose, like it was doing something. Ada lifted dumbbells and continued running. One day, just like that, she dropped down to 114 pounds of human flesh. Let me tell you, I've never almost flown that well since. Ada's shoulders became knives in her back, and her legs looked even longer than when she took ballet in her first semester and the instructor told her she'd need XL tights because her legs were that long. But yes, no, she was not eating. It wasn't important anymore, what happened to her body, not since I was there.

I appreciated it, of course—embodiment was luxurious, at least at first. I felt a new power, a flood of greatness that yes, Ada would regret later, valid, but for now it was good, rich; it meant I was an I, like I and I, like I wasn't going back to that larger we. Ha! How can? No, I was free. I had elevated, transcended, in fact. Risen like steam until it was me standing in the field of Ada's body. She named me this name, Asụghara, complete with that gritty slide of the throat halfway through. I hope it scrapes your mouth bloody to say it. When you name something, it comes into existence—did you know that? There is strength there, bone-white power injected in a rush, like a trembling drug.

Wait, is this how humans feel? To know that you are separate and special, to be individual and distinct? It's amazing. But I had to remind myself that I wasn't human or flesh. I was just a self, a little beast, if you like, locked inside Ada. Still, it was nice to be able to move her body and feel things. When I came in front, I moved like those masquerades from her childhood, with meat layered in front of my spirit face.

All I'm saying is, it was good to walk in the world.

I never forgot Virginia or the boy Soren—the place and person who midwifed me here. I also didn't forget that Ada was Ala's child. It would be too careless to forget something like that. If you are a python's child, then you are also a python—simple. There should have been a regular molting that came with that, but I was not regular. I wasn't allowed some gentle and slow shrugging off of skin. No, my own was to tear it away as soon as I came through, splitting it into pieces that were never found, coming out damp with blood. This is what happens when you act as if a human can hold godmatter without it curdling.

Ada loved me, sha. She loved me because I hated that boy. She loved me because I was reckless; I had no conscience, no sympathy, no pity. She loved me because I was strong and I held her together. I loved her because me, I had known her since I was nothing, since I was everything, since that shell-blue house in Umuahia. I loved her because I watched her grow up, because she gave offerings since I started awakening, feeding me from the crook of her arm and the skin of her thighs. Let me tell you now, I loved her because in the moment of her devastation, the moment she lost her mind, that girl reached for me so hard that she went completely mad, and I loved her because when I flooded through, she spread herself open and took me in without hesitation, bawling and broken, she absorbed me fiercely, all the way; she denied me nothing.

I loved her because she gave me a name.

Chapter Seven

[The ọgbanje are] creatures of God with powers over mortals. . . . They are not subject to the laws of justice and have no moral scruples, causing harm without justification.

—C. Chukwuemeka Mbaegbu,
The Ultimate Being in Igbo Ontology

Asụghara

After those days and nights of the boy fucking Ada's body, that summer in Georgia was my first embodied one, when I had Ada cut her hair in the sticky heat and wet air. Ada had gone down to stay with Itohan and her family like she always did every summer. Itohan's father used to work with Saachi, at the military hospitals they both got posted to. When Ada moved to America, Saachi asked if his family in Georgia could host Ada because she had nowhere else to go. It was too expensive to fly back to Nigeria and Saachi was still living overseas. Itohan's family agreed, and so Ada flew down and turned seventeen in their house. The mother and brothers lived out in the suburbs while Itohan, who Ada called her big sister, lived in an apartment complex that was more central, with hedges outside, carpet inside, and humidity pouring through the walls. I'm saying all of this to explain that these people were like family to Ada, so that when I tell you the kind of things I did after I arrived, you can understand the level of damage I caused.

I don't regret any of it, sha. I did what made me happy, whatever filled me up inside. I even remember one time, before I arrived, when Ada was talking to some friends in Virginia and she said, "You know, I'm glad that I haven't started having sex yet."

Her friends had laughed. "How come?" they asked, and Ada shrugged.

"It's just that if I start, I know how I'll get," she said. It's like she knew what kind of hunger I would arrive with, the way I would release it on an unprepared world if I ever made it past the veil. I don't know if she would have ever let me out, or if she had, if that would have been me, or something else. But I came into the world the way I did because of Soren, and whatever chance I had of being anything else was lost in that. I was a child of trauma; my birth was on top of a scream and I was baptized in blood. By the time Ada brought me to Georgia, I was ready to consume everything I touched.

I started with Itohan's younger brother. He was tall and beautiful, with smooth dark skin wrapped over muscle, but more importantly, he was there and it was easy. This was the first lesson I had learned from the third birth, about human men. I knew what they valued, I knew where they wanted to be, and I knew what price they would pay for a small death. So I fucked him on the short carpet of Itohan's apartment, a few feet away from the kitchenette where Ada ate frozen Tampico that she had mashed up in a plastic cup. I could almost see her standing aside as I used her body, stabbing the orange cubes with a metal teaspoon, the taste bringing Nigeria back into her mouth, memories of Fan-Orange she used to buy from the yogurt vendors who rode bicycles past her secondary school. I didn't care about her nostalgia; I had only been a seed then, it was a different world. My world now was the boy above and beneath me. I fucked him in the suburbs on the plain sheets of his bed, running Ada's fingernails down the tightness of his chest and stomach, amazed at how he could come and still stay hard. He snuck into the guest room of his mother's house to fuck me, where I cracked my hips open and faced away from him, and that was the only time I came.

Ada was never there. I had already promised; she would never be there, not again. It was my job to protect her. But I liked Itohan's brother, and I liked choosing a body for the first time. Soren didn't count—no one chose him. So I used Ada's face and practiced smiles on it, and to my surprise, Itohan's family couldn't tell the difference. I was that good. It's not difficult to pretend to be someone you've been watching since she was born, but I was a little insulted to be mistaken for Ada. She was so gullible: she went and threw herself right into the arms of people who broke her; she would see danger and instead of avoiding it like a person with sense, she would walk behind its teeth. As if she would be safe. As if her childhood shouldn't have taught her better. I refuse to believe that I looked anything like her—it must have been the humans who just couldn't tell the difference. Me, I made my mouth as red as silk, I turned my eyes black, and I made sure no one could trick me. When I did cruel things, I did them with my eyes open. I've never been ashamed—I always looked at myself without blinking. But as much as Ada loved me, she avoided meeting my gaze. We would both materialize in her mind, the marble room, cool veined white walls and floors, and she would look away. It was understandable: I had arrived and I was so deep inside her, locked into her flesh, moving her muscles. Suddenly she had to share with something she couldn't control. I understood, but at the same time, it wasn't my problem.

I was selfish back then. You can't really blame me—it was my first time having a body. Humans don't remember the time before they had bodies, so they take things for granted, but I didn't. I remembered not being myself, just being a piece of a cloud. I was careless with her body, sha, not thinking about the responsibilities of having flesh. Consequences were a thing that happened to humans, not to me. This was their world. I wasn't even really here. It's no excuse—I know I wasn't fair to Ada—but it was still a reason.

The first few times with Itohan's brother, he didn't wear a condom. When Ada brought it up, he was reluctant, he didn't want to go and buy them.

"Why on earth not?" Ada asked.

He looked uncomfortable. "If I buy them then it's like I know I'm going to sin, like I'm planning to go and have sex."

Ada stared at him. Inside her head, in the marble room, I came up and stood at her shoulder. We were thinking the exact same thing, and in that moment, it pulled us together, rippling electric.

I leaned over and spoke to her. "That's the stupidest thing I've ever heard."

She forgot to ignore me this time. "Be quiet. You know how religious they are."

"But it doesn't make any sense! He knows he's going to do it, so why is he pretending?" I asked, even though I already knew the answer. He was only a human—what else could I expect, realistically? He wanted to pretend he was somehow better than he knew he was; he wasn't ready to throw himself into sin. Humans find it easier to just lie and lie to themselves.

Ada made him get the condoms anyway, and he told her how awkward it had been when the cashier asked him what size he needed. I watched him tell the story, his mouth split into a shy smile through full lips, and I listened to Ada say whatever she was saying to him. Honestly speaking, I didn't care about the condoms, but then again, it wasn't my body. I should've cared, though, at least for Ada's sake.

What I cared about was that he felt good. Or maybe not good, but he made me feel full. He was thick and he stretched deep inside Ada, against the oath's velveteen, pushing her body open in a way that seemed to say, with confidence, you are alive and you have not died. For me, that was enough. Alive was flesh. Alive meant I had a body to move with.

Ada went with him to Planned Parenthood twice to get the morning-after pill, even after he bought the condoms. You see, she was the one who insisted on protection, but she was never the one he slept with—I was. On their second visit to the clinic, the nurse there looked at Ada with contempt.

"Maybe try using contraception?" she said, and her sarcasm brought blood rushing to Ada's cheeks.

"Don't mind her," I whispered to Ada, looking back at the woman with hatred. "Who is she, sef? Stupid bitch."

She's just a fucking human, I almost added, she doesn't even matter, none of this matters. Still, I didn't let Ada go back to the clinic after that, not even when it would have been the smart thing to do. There are many things I did to protect her and there are many ways in which I failed.

I continued to sleep with Itohan's brother, and one morning back at their mother's house in the suburbs, the sun was breaking like thin water through the window when Itohan's mother walked into the room and caught Ada lying inside the curve of the boy's long body. They were both wearing clothes—it was actually innocent, not like the night when Ada had been sleeping on the sofa in the upstairs parlor, when he held his penis to her face, thick and partial, bumping into her nose and nudging her lips apart. I had overtaken her before she woke up fully, moving quickly so I could push back the first wave of terror and disgust that was breaking in her. This was mine. He was mine. I had promised her, never again.

When his mother opened the door, Ada and the boy startled awake just in time to catch her firm gaze sweeping over them.

"Come to my room," she told her son, and shut the door with a sharp click.

Ada's stomach dropped. I stretched inside her and looked around lazily.

"Oh fuck," she said, sitting up. "Should I go also?"

"Shit." Itohan's brother leaped off the bed and pulled on a T-shirt. His face was twisted with worry. "Just stay here. I'm coming."

He left the room, carefully closing the door behind him as if someone else might walk past and see Ada in his sheets. I sat with her, excitement thudding through me. It was so bad, being caught. I loved it.

"What's going to happen?" Ada asked me, chewing on the corner of her thumb. "What if she finds out?"

I thought about it. "Well, what's the worst that could happen?"

"Don't be stupid," she said. "You know what will happen."

She was right. If Itohan's mother found out I had been fucking her third child under her roof, Ada wouldn't be welcome there anymore. Their family had wrapped her up as if she had a right to feel safe with them, and if this secret was discovered, she would lose them all.

"Don't worry," I told Ada. "She didn't see anything."

Ada wrapped her arm over her stomach. She was wearing an old oversized T-shirt, green with large colorful butterflies all over, a souvenir from the Philippines that Saachi had given her. She also wasn't really listening to me, not anymore; she was too afraid. I sat with her anyway, until the boy came back into the room looking chastened.

"She wants to talk to you," he said.

"What?!" Ada clambered off the bed. "For what? What did she say to you?"

He shrugged uncomfortably, not wanting to explain more. "Just go," he said. "She's waiting for you."

By then, even I had become cautious, although the thrill of being bad still hummed quietly in me. Ada walked down the short hallway and knocked on his mother's bedroom door, pushing it open when the woman's voice told her to come in. She had never been inside that room before. It was shadowed and Itohan's mother was sitting on the edge of her bed with a Bible lying next to her on the duvet. When she spoke, her voice was firm but not angry.

"I've seen you two cuddling on the couch before, and that one is fine," she said. "I know you weren't doing anything, but you should never share a bed with a man unless you are wearing his ring. Not even your own brother."

Ada kept a scared and straight face, but I caught her relief and broke out in rib-tearing laughter inside her.

"She doesn't know! I can't believe she doesn't know," I gasped. "Fuck!"

"Shut up," hissed Ada, her mouth closed.

The woman continued talking and my laughter turned bitter at how blind she was. So much had changed. So much had changed, and if this had happened six months before . . . but that wasn't even possible. Six months before, Ada would never have been in Soren's bed, I wouldn't have been born, and Ada would still be the sweet and good girl who this mother thought she was talking to. But I was here now and I was the world, lying in ugly entrails. I envied his mother the cleanliness she lived in, where everything was still innocent and no one had ever touched Ada. It was such a fucking lie.

After she released Ada from her room, Ada went back to the boy's bedroom, but she made sure to leave his door open. He was leaning against his wardrobe, looking beautiful and stressed out.

"I hate lying to my mother," he said.

Ada made a face and put her hand on his arm. "I know," she replied, and she meant it. She hated dishonesty and she knew what loving a mother felt like. Me, I rolled my eyes at the both of them.

"He can hate what he wants," I told her. "You know he loves fucking us. It's not as if he's going to stop. They never stop."

"You mean he loves fucking you," she whispered back, and I made a rough sound. She was right. I was staying behind her face like a good little spirit, sha, like a small beast on a leash. When the boy drove us to church, Ada stood up in the car to stick her head out of the sunroof and feel the wind rocketing against her face.

"Come inside the car," he scolded.

She looked down at his face and sat back in her seat. "What's the problem?"

He stared straight ahead, through the windshield, his face set. "My girlfriend won't do things like that."

Ada raised her eyebrows and I snorted inside her head, but neither of us said anything. After the service, Ada headed toward the other car to return to the house with the rest of the family—the boy had to run some errands.

"You people, take care of my wife," he called out to his mother and his sister and his older brother. His voice carried over the green lawn and he was smiling like the sun, and everyone laughed fondly as Ada blushed.

After I had Ada cut off her hair, the boy was disapproving, but he still prayed with Ada when he dropped her off at the airport because he had somehow become her boyfriend. When he prayed, Ada held his hands, closed her eyes, and pretended as if she could feel Yshwa anywhere close to her. She couldn't, of course, not anymore, but I was helping her get better at lying.

After her visit with Saachi, Ada flew back to Virginia for her final year at the university. On her first day back, she walked through the cafeteria and set her tray down on a table. One of her friends on the track team slid in next to her, flipping a ponytail over her shoulder.

"Hey, Ada. How was your summer?"

Ada shrugged. "It was cool. Went to Georgia, visited my mother, had sex. You know, the usual."

Her friend shrieked. Everyone knew Ada had never been touched like that before. "Girl, what?! You got laid?"

Ada smiled and they both dissolved into laughter.

Her friend was nodding and proud. "Yo, when I saw you walking across the room, I could tell, you know? I said, 'Yeah, she's walking different.'"

I wondered if that was true. Was I showing that much on the outside? Had I entered Ada's walk, the way she moved her head, her smile? She kept stretching her mouth and laughing with them, but I knew she was just relieved that they were treating her as if she was normal, now that she wasn't the uptight virgin anymore. But inside, I could smell it: she still felt ashamed, dirty with sin. She hadn't gone back to her christ, Yshwa. Instead she went to see that other boy she'd been talking to over the summer, that other brother of a friend, the one who was there when she left Soren. Ada thought she might love this new boy. If she could love Soren, then why not this one? But while I was kissing him on the blue mattress of Ada's dorm room, I drifted her hand down between his legs and recoiled at the thinness of his penis.

"I can't work with that," I told Ada, and I ended the crush.

She didn't argue with me. I had her call Itohan's younger brother, and she broke up with him.

"I was feeling single already," he said. He sounded petulant.

"Good," I told Ada. "It's better this way."

"If you say so," she said, and she let him go.

The next summer, we went back to Georgia, and I set my sights on Itohan's older brother. Ada never forgave me for what I did to him.

* * *

She wasn't doing a lot of forgiving, to be fair. Not of me, not of herself. Before Soren, Ada had been obsessed with her christ, that Yshwa. She loved him, or to be more accurate, she adored and worshipped him, which is exactly how he likes it. She lived for him. I don't even know why—he was never there for her, not like me, not even close. He couldn't even be bothered to materialize when she was just a little girl, when she really, really needed him. How can you leave a child alone like that? But whatever—it's stupid to think that gods actually care about you. Ada stopped talking to him after I was born, all because of that promise she'd made to be abstinent, which is another thing I don't understand. Her body meant more to me than it ever did to her. Promising abstinence was like promising not to play with a weapon that she didn't even like in the first place. After Soren was done with her, Ada walked away from Yshwa and straight into my arms, where she belonged. Yshwa's teachings included a lot about repentance and forgiveness and being white as the snow of a bleached lamb, the general gist being that you could fuck up and start over, and Ada believed in it until I was born and then she didn't.

She tried to, since it seemed like a betrayal to lose faith so deeply, to be that lost, but she just couldn't believe that she would ever be clean again. Now that I was there, with my sleek skin and wet hair, she was probably right. I couldn't be excised. Life moves in only one direction and things couldn't go back to what they used to be: bright and untouched, with Ada being ignorant of what our shared body now meant and what it could be used for.

All that mattered was this, and I told her—I had to use the body first, before they did.

Yshwa didn't give up on Ada, which was touching, I suppose. He started to materialize inside her mind, as if he was one of us, as if he belonged there. He was trying to reach her but I never liked him, so I blocked him at every chance. He had too much light inside him, it was always reflecting off the marble and glaring into my eyes. I would have to pull in shadows just to soak it all up. But it wasn't difficult to keep him away from Ada; she didn't believe him anyway, that he would take her back. Yshwa kept trying to tell her what it would take her three years to hear, that she hadn't done anything wrong, but she was so hurt and broken that she heard nothing. The only one who was listening to him was me, and he could tell I didn't care. Yshwa had this way of looking at me, with this half-loving, half-sad face, his head tilted to one side and darkness drifting off his shoulders from the shadows I tried to throw on him.

"I'm just trying to help her, you know." His voice was tucked and soft. I didn't care.

"I don't care," I told him. "Just go away."

"I want to help you too. I can help you too."

"I don't need your help. Go away."

"Asụghara," he said, and my name sounded like a spring bubbling in his mouth.

I glimmered in and out impatiently. He was sitting cross-legged on the marble, wearing bone-colored linens, his hair short and curled this time. I stood by her eyes, looking out, dressed in matte black. The shadows were good at sticking to me.

"Do you really think what you're doing with Ada is helping?" he asked, and I could feel my temper growing my nails out, long and pointed, dark red like his blood an hour after they pierced his side. I folded my arms and stared at him. I wanted him to leave.

"Are you angry with me?" he asked.

"I don't want you here," I told him. "You make her sad. You remind her of too much shit. You know I don't give a fuck about you, but you still matter to her, and this"—I gestured at his presence on my marble—"all this does is make it harder. For her."

He looked at me as if I was a wound. "You're so far away from home," he said, so quietly that I thought he was talking to himself. Then he added, "I'm not leaving her. You understand?"

"Then you're an idiot," I snapped. "It doesn't matter whether you say you're leaving her or not. You don't want to hear word—Ada is not talking to you anymore."

"She talks to me all the time," Yshwa shot back. "She's crying, she's screaming, the girl is sorry all the time. There's so much guilt over her eyes, it covers everything else."

I scoffed at him. Gods always think everything is about them. "Biko, that's not talking. That's basically her telling you good-bye. As in, you're behind her while I'm in front. In fact, I'm around her. I'm everywhere. She tells me what she's too ashamed to tell you."

"*You* are the thing she's ashamed of," he reminded me. "And I hear everything anyway."

I was amazed at how well I was keeping my temper. "Clap for yourself. She's still not talking to you. So go away."

He stood up, towering above me. "I'll be here, Asụghara. Ada knows that."

"She has me." I couldn't help snarling at him when I said it. "It's enough."

Yshwa touched my cheek and his palm felt like wet silk. "I'm not ashamed of you," he said, as if it was nothing. "You know I love you."

I jerked my head away. "Fuck you."

He gave me that damn look again as he left, the fucking resurrected bastard, but I didn't care, I was just glad that he was gone. He wasn't getting her back. Ada was mine, I told myself, standing in the empty marble.

She was mine.

Chapter Eight

The back of your brain is open.

We

Allow us to interject; these births are complicated moltings, leaving skins all over the place. But remain assured, Asụghara's presence was not our absence, never that. We fell back when she burst forward, true, but we are many and she was just one of us, a beastself, a weapon that needed to be put in play. We let her mount the Ada, we let that story ride out—it has as many layers as we do. Here is one of them: the story of the other gods.

We have told you about some of them—Yshwa, for example. Ala, the controller of minor gods, our mother. But there are others, and anyone who knows anything knows this, knows about the godly stowaways that came along when the corrupters stole our people, what the swollen hulls carried over the bellied seas, the masks, the skin on the inside of the drum, the words under the words, the water in the water. The stories that survived, the new names they took, the temper of old gods sweeping through new land, the music taken that is the same as the music left behind. And, of course, the humans who survived, those selected among them, the ones in white, the ones shaking shells and mineral deposits, the ones ridden, the ones chosen, the ones who follow, work, and serve because calls pass through blood no matter how many oceans you drop death into.

Those humans recognized us easily; it was as if they could smell us under the Ada's skin or feel us in the air that heaved around her. After the Ada left home and got tucked into that little town in the mountains, she met one of them, the Dominican girl with the cigars. Her name was Malena and she was a daughter of Changó, of Santa Bárbara. She met the Ada at a meeting for the community service fraternity they'd both joined, before the Ada met Soren, before Asụghara arrived in the third birth-skinning.

The two of them, Malena and the Ada, used to sit out on the redbrick porches of the old school buildings and smoke cigars together, listening to the sharp breaking calls of Dominican palos pierce the air on the humped backs of drums and seedsounds. On one of those nights, we flung ourselves through the Ada's body, dancing to the words we could and could not hear, dark air around us. Malena watched us with slitted eyes, a cigar in her red and white mouth, smoke wrapping her face.

On another night, Malena's body was there but Malena was gone, and a mansaint with a deep voice used the muscles of her mouth. He gave the Ada a message to give to Malena for when she got her body back, something we can't remember now, but that is expected: the message was for Malena and not for us, after all. When the Ada passed it on, Malena was unfazed; it was normal for her, to be mounted and then left by saints, gods, spirits. The Ada was amazed but we were respectful. We loved Malena because she smelled like us.

But all these new things changed nothing; we were still ọgbanje, and back home, our brothersisters held many angers against us—for being born incorrectly, for not returning, for crossing the ocean sifted with death. Nevertheless, we were still one of them. None of their grievances would ever change that and they knew it, so they sent us messages, reminders of who we were, bread crumbs for when the Ada would unblock her ears and understand the weight stitched inside her stomach. They pushed her toward Malena, they put words under Malena's tongue.

"There's a claim on your head, Ada," she told us. "Back home. Something wants you back home."

"Who?" The Ada didn't know the things we did. None of this sounded like anything to her.

"I don't know." Malena pushed her black hair off her face and poured a glass of Johnnie Walker. "These are West African gods, not mine, so I can't speak to them like that, you know?"

She told us other things, though. "You're the daughter of Santa Marta," she said, early on. "La Dominadora."

The Ada looked her up online and we all gazed at the imported image on the computer screen: a mirrored forest of black hair springing from the scalp, the scaled lengths of our mother's ambassadors wrapped around Santa Marta's hands. It was all the same, a million mothers with a million names all flicking their quick tongues over the clear path to our spine.

We wondered—what would Ala have said to Malena's claim that Santa Marta was the Ada's mother? An old god to a newer, younger one. Santa Marta, the one who raises the wind and uncovers the bones, while the humans throw up circular pinnacles of clay in Ala's name, raking five rows in the earth on either side. Ala, the god that gives children with both hands and watches them multiply like leaves creeping over the earth, seven seas roaring under her feet. Perhaps she would call Santa Marta by her other name, Filomena Lubana, and warn her not to send her husband into the Ada's dreams. San Elias, El Barón del Cementerio, the Baron. Whoever guards the underworld guards Ala's womb, you see; they are the same place. The Baron stepped over an island and into twenty-one rivers to put his name on the Ada's tongue, so she called it out. (What do you do when a lwa wants you? No, that is a different story—forget the Baron.) It would be a warning, we decided, Ala to Filomena Lubana, a warning that the child was not hers. Nine Marta bore and nine Marta buried. The Ada has always belonged to Ala, and Ala is not inclined to share. Take away those brown eggs and honey.

In Virginia, Malena watched clotted scratches and cuts erupt on the Ada's arms. She talked to her saints and her saints spoke to her.

"They told me you were going to kill yourself," she said to the Ada, years later. "When we were in school. You remember? You started breaking glass, cutting yourself? Yeah. That was them." Cigar smoke. Whiskey mouth. "Your African, he was on top of you and you just couldn't shake him. You were telling me that you just couldn't do it anymore."

The Ada listened while on a slow train pulling itself through the desert of the Southwest, away from Saachi's house, toward the Pacific. Malena was in New York, deep in Queens, her voice ten years familiar by then.

"I saved your life, Ada." She never told the Ada what exactly she'd worked or what the rituals looked like, only that they were necessary. "I held a lot of stuff that was gonna hurt you," she said. "The problem is that when you have saints, old-school saints, trying to communicate with you, they don't understand. It's like talking to your grand-grand-granddaddy about the Internet."

We wondered why Malena watched us, why she cared, who had sent her. "Thank you," said the Ada, smiling into the phone, her head resting on the ruined Amtrak glass.

"You crazy?" Malena scoffed, thousands of miles packed into it. "I love you. I would do whatever for you to be there in my life. I didn't want to tell you because at the end of the day you're my sister and what I wouldn't do for my sister and my blood."

She paused to shout in Spanish at someone on her side of the connection and came back to the line, her voice firm.

"You would've done it for me."

It is like we said, we loved her, from back when we all lived in the mountains, for the way she loved us, all of us, and never made the Ada feel insane. For the way she was a witness. She worked for the other gods, yes, but she loved us and perhaps she did help save the Ada; perhaps what she worked was part of the veil-tearing that brought Asụghara here, the third birth. We do not know these other gods, so we cannot verify the impact of what their workers wrought. It was a small mercy, though, to be around those humans who could see us flashing beneath the Ada's skin. The worst part of embodiment is being unseen. When the Ada got married, perhaps it would have been better if she married someone like that. But she was insisting on being human and she married a human. He was a force of a human, true, with storm eyes and hands like a future, but he was still just a human.

We should have saved her for a god.

Chapter Nine

Mgbe nnukwu mmanwụ pụta, obele mmanwụ na-agba ọsọ.

Ada

I don't even have the mouth to tell this story. I'm so tired most of the time. Besides, whatever they will say will be the truest version of it, since they are the truest version of me. It's a strange thing to say, I know, considering that they made me mad. But I am not entirely opposed to madness, not when it comes with this kind of clarity. The world in my head has been far more real than the one outside—maybe that's the exact definition of madness, come to think of it. It's all a secret I've had to keep, but no longer, not since you're reading this. And it should all make sense; I didn't want to be alone, so I chose them. In many ways, you see, I am not even real.

When they speak so contemptuously of humans, I'm never sure if they mean me as well. Sometimes I wonder if there even is a me without them. They talk about Ewan, the man I married, as if he was nothing, because he was only flesh. But I loved him and that made him more than human to me. Love is transformative in that way. Like small gods, it can bring out the prophet in you. You find yourself selling dreams of spectacular hereafters, possible only if you believe, if you really, really believe. So in loving Ewan, he somehow became a god. I don't mean that in a good way—he made me suffer but I still cast idols in his name, as people have done for their gods for millennia. It didn't end there. When the years accumulated and exposed Ewan's cracks, I covered them in gold and bronze. That's what you do for the idols you make. But I loved him, I really did, and he loved me, and that was the danger—is there any story of a human loving a god that ends well? I was so busy pretending I was normal back then, I didn't know enough to think of that. So maybe he made me suffer, but how much can flesh really hurt spirit? Who do you think will be bruised more in the end?

You see, you've gone and caught me. I'm talking as if I'm them. It's all right. In many ways, I am not even real. I am not even here.

Chapter Ten

Do you feel real when he touches you or do you still feel dead?

Asụghara

I wasn't born when Ada met Ewan, but I can tell the story anyway. And I'm even glad I wasn't there. It's good that Ada had that for herself, before the rest of us got to her.

Like me and Soren, Ewan happened in Virginia. It was winter and there was a party at the tennis house, bodies pressing in a crush downstairs and music thudding against the plaster of the walls. Ada had gone upstairs to one of the bedrooms, where the noise faded away into strains of reggae and blue light filtering through a computer screen. Ewan was sitting on the bed with his back to the wall, but she had no idea who he was; she'd never seen or noticed him before that night. A friend introduced them and Ewan was easy, charming, comfortable. Soon Ada was sitting next to him, both of them chatting as people came in and out of the room, smoke softening the air around them. Ewan was Irish, green-eyed, the star of the tennis team. When they tentatively held hands, Ada smiled nervously. She was only eighteen and she was still sweet.

"My mother thinks my palms are rough," she said. Ada didn't feel delicate—she never had. At fourteen, she couldn't fit into dresses Saachi wore when she was twenty-five.

Ewan ran his thumb over her life line. "No," he said, looking at her as if she was wedding crystal. "They're very soft."

Ada blushed. She stayed with him until the friends she came with were ready to leave. The next day was a Saturday and, as usual, everyone ended up at Gilligan's. Ada kept looking around for Ewan as the night wore in and around, but he didn't show up and her heart sank. It began to climb again, cautiously, when she ran into one of his roommates as the club was closing out, and, giddy with luck, caught a ride back to the tennis house. She hung out with them upstairs, trying to seem casual when she was really waiting and hoping. Finally, Ewan wandered into the room and smiled to see her.

"I had a feeling it was you," he said, and took her down to his room, where she taught him to play cards with Maxwell playing in the background. It was four in the morning, but Ada had gotten what she wanted, to see him. She always got what she wanted, even before I showed up. There was a framed photograph of a girl in a graduation gown on his dresser, but Ada didn't ask any questions. She knew enough to avoid certain answers, and the moment with Ewan was too significant to disturb with whatever his actual life held. All that mattered was that he made her laugh and that there was so much peace with him, she could almost see it in the air. When he leaned in to kiss her, she tasted sharp smoke in his flesh and she could see the starkness of his skin against hers. It was her first time kissing a white person, and briefly, she wondered why he didn't have any lips. He didn't seem real, from the thick richness of his voice and the weight of his rolled consonants to the things about his life that sounded as if they were pulled from the Frank McCourt memoirs she'd read as a child. He felt like an escape, so Ada spent the night wrapped up and tucked in his arms while he played Al Green to her. *We're dying today,* she thought. *I could do this for almost forever.*

She went back to her dorm room in the morning. It was finals week, so she continued studying, and in the afternoon, she ran into Ewan in the library. He leaned out of his carrel to share his earphones with her.

"Listen to this," he said, and played her some Amos Lee. Ada wrote down the name of the song and then Ewan kissed her cheek and left.

In the evening, she went to a final exhibit for a photography class because she'd modeled for one of her friends in the class and she knew Juan, another of the photography students. He was from Mexico, slim and brown and beautiful. He used to live in the house down the hill with Luka, and he burned packs and packs of India Temple incense. One evening, he and Ada had sat together and talked about how amazing it would be if either of them could play the violin. Juan had laughed and tilted his head back. "I'd just sit on my porch with a bowl of weed and play it all day, man." He'd held an imaginary bow and moved it against imaginary strings, and Ada had wished that all of it was real, that she was on that porch with him and the music and nothing else.

At the exhibit, when they lifted up the first of Juan's prints, Ada nearly choked. Every photograph was of Ewan.

The air around her thickened. As they placed each print on the lighted ledge, a weight began to press on her, crushing her with colors and reflections and textures. She remembered everything she thought she'd forgotten from the previous nights: the scarf around Ewan's neck with the forest-green clover in the corner, smoke wreathing up from his mouth, the taste of it from his lips and tongue. She glanced around the room, wondering if anyone could tell how affected she was by the photographs. Ewan had left for the winter break already. He was gone, and now she was left behind, asphyxiating on his image.

Much later, I would discover that Ewan always tasted like a drug, even in his absences. But that night, it was Ada who lay on her bed in her dorm room and let the rush of him stretch out her veins. Ewan felt like a better madness to her than anything else had before. She rolled over on her stomach and pulled out her diary to write to him, since he was not there.

"I'm returning to sanity," she wrote, "to the real world. But I will never forget how it felt to be overwhelmed by your beauty. You made me feel so alive and so right, and I know that in the real world, I will feel nothing for you and I will move on, and we'll follow these rules because when it comes down to survival, we have to. I envy your girl, the one who holds your heart. If you ever need to take a break from this world, call me. I will come to you in a heartbeat and we will steal time."

Ewan didn't come back the next semester.

Ada e-mailed him through his school e-mail and, after weeks, gave up on him replying. Classes began without him, the parties thudded through the houses and he wasn't there, and quickly enough, everything she'd felt with him stopped feeling even faintly real. You can't really sustain a madness like that without its object's presence. Ada soon had other problems to deal with anyway. There was Soren, and then there was me, my loud birth, the summer in Georgia, and then we all came back to Virginia. The August heat was beating through the glass windows of the school gym when Ada saw Ewan again. I was inside the marble room when I felt her heart shake and I turned my head sharply to look at him.

"Wait," I said. "Who's that?"

"Nobody," she said, smiling as she said hello and walked past. "A ghost. Don't mind him."

I looked back at him as we walked away. "You know you can't lie to me. Is he important?"

Ada took a deep breath. "We'll see."

I was curious. I went to her memories and looked up everything I needed to know. She didn't think much of his return, that part was true. Too much had happened, too much hurt.

But that Saturday, Ada was at Gilligan's and Ewan stopped her on the dance floor, drunk, his accent tumbling out with force.

"You're the classiest person I've met at this school," he said. "Come by the house. We'll listen to music again."

Ada watched the back of his head as he left. She was thoughtful. By then, she was more used to me, since we had just spent our first few months together. I liked that because with me there, it meant that she was less alone. "What do you think?" she asked me.

I didn't even need to consider it. "Oh, I think we should go," I said, a bit selfishly, since I just wanted to see for myself if that chemistry in her memory was the real thing, if the two of them could make it happen again. Anyone who felt like a drug was a person I was interested in. Ever since I dropped the one with the thin penis, I had been so bored. I missed having toys to play with.

A few days later, we walked down the hill to the house Ewan had moved to, up the street from Luka. Ada was nervous because she wasn't exactly sure if she would be welcome there. Ewan had been drunk when he invited her—maybe he hadn't meant it. At the house, the boys had just come back from practice, rackets and sweat everywhere.

"Oh god," Ada whispered to me as we stepped through the doorway. "What am I doing here?"

"Hold on," I said, pressing against her eyes. "There he is."

Ewan looked up from the couch he was on and sprang to his feet, welcoming Ada with a surprised smile. He hadn't expected her to show up but was clearly glad that she did. I watched, fascinated, as they left the house and walked to Main Street, down to the coffee shop, where he and Ada sat as she played him Nina Simone through a shared set of earphones. The mountains were tall and green around them. I sat in Ada and didn't interfere, minding my own business for once.

She never gave him the number to her dorm room and they never e-mailed or planned anything. Ada would just walk down that hill with the grass brushing her ankles, cool sunshine on her head, his room at the end of her journey. They would listen to music, talk, and then she started spending the night once in a while, lying in his arms under three comforters when the weather turned cold. His bed was a mattress lodged behind a dresser and braced against the wall. They didn't even kiss. I don't know why I left them alone—maybe I felt she had more of a right to him because she met him before I was born. But he was different, you know; he was not someone I needed to hunt. He meant her no harm. He didn't even try to touch her. So I could, for a while at least, allow it to continue.

On Wednesdays they danced against the bar at the Irish pub, and on Saturdays, on the dance floor at Gilligan's. Ewan loved Ada's short hair and she compared that with Itohan's younger brother, who had told her with disgust that she would look like a boy. With Ewan, they just listened to music and talked about their childhoods, and it was all nice and innocent if you forget that they were humans who had hearts. Eventually, they started to wonder what exactly they were doing, and that's how they ended up on the couch in Ewan's room, both nervous and unsure.

"I have a girlfriend," he said.

"I know," said Ada. They looked at each other.

"I've cheated on her before, with other girls."

They had avoided either of these truths because that was the real world, the one that wasn't supposed to infringe on their bubble. Bringing it up scared the shit out of Ada. She didn't want to be out there alone, so she reached for me. I came in, but I entered gently because it wasn't time to fight yet. She just needed a little coldness, a pinch of ruthlessness. I looked back at Ewan with her eyes. "Okay?" I said.

"I can't do it with you," he explained. "It would be different, I already know. I would care too much, get emotionally attached." His words were floating up toward the old ceiling.

Inside the marble room, I looked at Ada and she shook her head. She wasn't looking for anything. She didn't believe in that anymore.

"Are you sure?" I asked her.

She shrugged, wrapping her arms around herself. "I found him and he makes me happy. That's enough for me. Who needs a forever?"

I nodded. "No wahala. Whatever you want."

I turned back to him. "I don't want a relationship from you," I said, as if none of it was a big deal. I was cool, languid, casual. "I like you. You like me. It's that simple."

Ewan laughed and Ada smiled back at him and the bubble stayed safe. In his bed that night, Ewan held her face and kissed her for all the time they had waited. When Ada kissed him back, it was very different from their first kiss, the one that happened before I was born. She hadn't known desire then. This time, she had me, and he had come back, and so she drank smoke from his mouth like it was air. I barely even had to be there.

His girlfriend remained a pale face in a picture frame on his dresser. Ada continued to flow through Ewan's life: nothing holding her, nothing keeping her, nothing pushing her away. One night at the Irish pub, she danced to a Shakira song with a Brazilian friend, their hips intimate, moving in a way a white boy's couldn't. Ewan smiled at her from the bar where he was standing with his friends.

"I wasn't in the least bit jealous, you know," he told her afterward, when she was back in his arms.

"Why not?" she asked.

Ewan smiled again, assured. "I know it's me you like."

He was right. Still, for a while all they did after these nights out was curl up in his bed, make out, and then sleep. Everyone knew about them. His best friend couldn't believe they hadn't fucked yet. Even me, sef—sometimes I couldn't believe we hadn't fucked yet. Luka had pulled back from Ada because he and Ewan were good friends and it was clear who she'd chosen. I knew it was the right choice. Everything with Ewan was moving at a different pace, one I wasn't interfering with, one that no one had given Ada before. I wasn't going to fuck that up for her. My job was just to be there if she needed me. Besides, I liked Ewan. He was a typical bad boy, after all—older, popular, a writer who drank all the time and smoked weed and cigarettes and blacked out regularly. Ada was the model student—she was both president of her graduating class and, at nineteen, the youngest person in it. Everyone at the school, like in Georgia, only saw her and couldn't see me. It was fine. No wahala. They didn't need to see me for me to be who I was.

One night, Ewan turned to Ada at the pub. "We have unfinished business," he said, his eyes wrinkling as he smiled. If she didn't know what he meant, I did. I know how to recognize my cues. But Ada didn't mind. She liked him and I liked him, so it all worked out. Except that Ada was still Ada and I was still me, and this was where we overlapped. She didn't have a capacity for desire that ran deep enough for fucking, she never did. Ada has been consistent. When it came to things like that, she came to me. We are the same person, you get? So that night, when Ewan took off her clothes, me, I took my place under her skin. I had made her a promise. I do not make exceptions.

She fell in love with him weeks later. I get annoyed just remembering it. I had been having a fantastic time with Ewan before that because, as it turned out, he had a dark side too, one that looked like me, a cruel and ruthless thing. I saw it one night when his eyes were cold and his voice was flat, when he covered Ada's mouth with a rough hand as he fucked me. When he was done, he got off the bed and tossed a towel at Ada, lighting a cigarette. Ada didn't say anything and Ewan turned away from her on the bed, closing his eyes. "Come on," I told her, and I had her put on her shoes in the heavy dark and leave quietly.

It was Halloween a few days later and Ada showed up to the party at Ewan's house dressed as me, wearing a black corset, a tiny black skirt, knee-high boots, and shining skin. Her friends leaned in, laughing.

"And what are you supposed to be?" they asked.

I grinned back at them with her teeth. "Whatever you want," I said.

I had Ada walk straight to Ewan's room, depositing her body on his lap. He wrapped a freckled arm around her as people flowed in and out of his doorway.

"I've been feeling bad about what I'm doing to my girlfriend," he confessed.

Oh fuck, I thought, *feelings*. I wonder how the conversation would have gone if he could have reached Ada in that moment. She probably would have reciprocated; she always responded to honesty and vulnerability, she was sweet like that. But I had her body that night, and so he had to deal with me and I really hate when people talk about feelings.

"Is that why you were all fucking weird the other night?" I asked. He made a face and I shoved my finger into his ribs. "I don't need that nonsense. Next time you're in a mood like that, just don't fuck me at all."

Ewan stayed serious and looked into Ada's eyes, his voice matter-of-fact. "What you and I have, it's more than fucking," he said. "I'm basically in a relationship with you."

I swore to myself when he said that—I could already feel Ada's heart pounding. Stupid, stupid girl.

I turned inward for a moment, just to deal with her. She was twisting her hands together in the marble room, his words still ringing against the walls. "No," I said, before she could get a word out. "Don't even fucking think about it."

"But, Asụghara, he just said—"

"No!" I glared at her and she fell silent. I could see I was crushing her, but there was no other option. I couldn't allow her hope any room to breathe; I had to choke it out. I was protecting her.

"Allow me to handle this," I told her. "Stay here."

I turned back out and gave Ewan a sharp look, keeping my voice loose but cutting. "That's too bad for you," I said. "Because I'm not in a relationship with anyone."

Ewan laughed and shook his head. He looked tired. It was not the last time he would look for Ada only to be met with me.

"So, what do you want to do?" I asked him. "You want to stop?"

He looked up at me and shifted his face, locking away his emotions, returning to the way I liked him. "It's Halloween and I've got a horny nineteen-year-old in a slutty black costume sitting in my lap," he said. He was twenty-seven then. "What do you think?"

"Good," I answered, and kissed him with Ada's mouth. I wasn't done playing with him. It was ideal—Ada didn't have time to think about Soren or what he'd done, even though she was back on the same campus where it happened. I had barely thought about my own birth myself. I was busy trying out new toys, like getting Ada drunk for the first time. Had I known earlier how useful alcohol would be in lubricating my relationship with Ada and bringing us together, I would have stocked her life with bottles. But that first time happened completely by accident—she drank too many Smirnoff Ices on an empty stomach, because I was still having her starve herself, and she was already halfway drunk by the time she agreed to try some margaritas at the club.

Ewan wasn't out with her that night, so Ada's friends dropped her off at his house after the club. It was winter, but she was wearing a flared miniskirt and black boxer boots. It was three in the morning and Ewan's door was bolted shut from inside his room. His housemates were still awake, but Ada didn't want to talk to any of them; she just wanted to sleep. It was too cold to walk up the hill to her dorm, and their living room was filthy, so she couldn't crash on a couch. She banged on his door and called his name, but Ewan didn't answer.

"You know he's drunk and passed out," I told her. "Biko, just kick the fucking door down."

I liked drunk Ada because instead of arguing, she actually agreed with me. She needed to sleep, his room was the solution, and the door was an obstacle that needed to be removed. Simple. She'd also taken karate lessons all semester, so it was perfect. The alcohol made her more like me, cold and steady, and Ada timed her roundhouse kicks to land with precision on the painted wood of his door.

The noise brought Ewan's best friend downstairs. "What the fuck's going on?"

Ada waved her hand at the door. "Ewan's passed out and I need to sleep, so I'm kicking it down," she explained. I giggled inside her.

The best friend looked from Ada to the door, then nodded. "Okay." He held out one of the McDonald's sandwiches he was holding. "Want one?"

They ate and talked, and Ada excused herself to smash her heel into the door every few minutes. I am still not sure how much of her was me that night, to be honest, but I can tell you it was a lot more than usual. We were synched and it was beautiful.

The bolt to Ewan's room went into the wall, so when the door finally broke, it did so at its hinges, the doorframe cracking and shuddering as it gave way. Ada squeezed through the small space and climbed into bed with Ewan. He cracked open sleepy blue eyes to smile at her.

"Unbelievable," I muttered at him. "Breaking down the door doesn't wake you up, but me climbing into bed does."

In the morning, Ada woke up sober and with her first hangover. When she realized what had happened, she was so horrified that she couldn't stop apologizing to Ewan. He thought it was hilarious. So did all his friends, but for different reasons. They spread the story that Ada had been so desperate to fuck Ewan that she broke his door down. Ada found it humiliating, but I took some of that feeling away for her. The rumors didn't matter. Those people didn't matter—shit, barely anyone mattered. The broken door stayed propped up until Ewan moved out of that house. No one ever fixed it.

Everything wore down into a cycle. Ewan drank and smoked like he was dying. Ada drank tequila, now that I'd discovered that it made her sink deeper into me. She and Ewan fucked and partied and rinsed and repeated. I started to come out more and more. On the porch of Luka's house, sitting with Malena, I discovered that I could put out a cigar on Ada's palm and a blister would rise. Malena just shook her head at me. She was the witness—she was the only person who saw me through Ada's skin—and I loved her for that. I had Ada switch from Malena's cigars to thin chocolate cigarillos, and she would smoke them as she walked down the hill to Ewan's house, leaving a faint taste of cocoa on her lips. He woke up one night to find me standing in his room in the darkness, watching him in Ada's body, a dark silhouette with a glowing red light at my mouth.

He called me the devil. I didn't mind. I'd heard that before. I wondered if he noticed when he lost her and got me instead.

"It's scary when I make all your fantasies come true, isn't it?" I told him.

He should never have touched her if he wanted to keep her, but how could he know? Humans. Still, I shouldn't have been surprised that Ada fell in love with him. She read the stories he wrote, he kissed her hand on their nights out and told her how lucky he was to have her, how lucky he was that she chose him. I didn't disagree—he was right, he was lucky to have us. Ada cooked dinners for him and his housemates, and they sat around the dining table, loud and lovely, eating dhal and Malaysian parathas. It felt like, between me and her, we knew both sides of him—the bright and the dark, the kind and the cruel, one for each of us. We knew what he was capable of, something his faraway girlfriend didn't. Anyway, Ada went and fell in love and decided to tell him, and I didn't stop her because she would have quarreled with me about it. Love does people like that. It was easier to just let her go ahead—I could shield her from whatever the outcome was.

They were lying in his bed as she stammered it out, her sentences breaking as she tried to remember what he'd told her recently, that it didn't matter what anyone else thought, that they were the only ones who mattered. Ewan was patient, his face close to hers, breathing in her exhalations, holding her against him as she looked for the courage to break her own heart.

"If you ever make me feel stupid for saying this, I will kill you," Ada said, her eyes stinging. Ewan smiled a little and she squeezed her eyes shut, taking a deep breath. "I love you," she whispered, and then the sadness rushed in. "I'm sorry. I know it's not what we agreed, I know I only asked you to never lie to me and never make me feel cheap, and you've kept your side of the bargain and I haven't and I'm sorry. It's just that I don't want anyone who's not you."

"Hey, hey. It's okay." Ewan brushed his fingers over the side of her face. "I already knew you were going to say that, and I know it took a lot of courage. When you feel strongly about something, it's a good thing to let it out."

He didn't say it back. Of course he didn't say it back. This isn't that kind of story. But he held Ada for a long time, lying on his back with her head on his shoulder. The night grew deeper. I sat alone in the marble and let her have this with him.

"You can turn to your side," Ada whispered. "I know that's how you need to sleep."

Ewan kissed her forehead. "Shut up," he said. "Stop trying to take care of everyone else."

Everyone left for Christmas break soon after. Ada went to Saachi and Añuli and said nothing about Ewan because there was nothing to say. When she came back to Virginia, she ran into him at Gilligan's and his eyes lit up. They stood by the bar and caught up, leaning toward each other to shut out the rest of the noise.

"I wanted to get you this CD I saw, but I thought it was too cliché to give the African girl a CD with African music on it," Ewan told her, and she laughed. They stayed in the club until they'd both missed their rides.

"Let's just walk," he suggested. It was three miles back to his house and he held Ada's hand the whole way as he told her about his girlfriend, how much he adored her, that they'd talked about breaking up.

"You told me once that you're more honest with me than you ever were with her," Ada said.

Ewan nodded. "Probably true," he said.

They kept walking and Ada looked up at the largeness of the sky. It was strange, she thought, to be here in Virginia, with this man, inside this bubble they'd built.

"What kind of parents do you think we'd be?" she asked.

Ewan thought for a moment. "I think if a guy came up and said outright, 'I'm fucking your daughter,' we'd probably just look at each other—"

"—and shrug—" added Ada.

"—and say, 'You know what? Fair enough.'" They laughed as they crossed a road and cut through a parking lot. "Can you imagine what our kid would look like?"

"What, brown skinned with freckles?" said Ada, giggling.

"And a ginger afro." Ewan bent over laughing, and I watched them both from inside her head, amused. It was cute. They talked about how their families would receive them—they talked as if things weren't impossible, as if choices hadn't already been made. I didn't interfere, not yet. When they got to his room and got into bed, Ada hesitated.

"We don't have to do anything," she said. "Things have changed, you know, we can step back and just be friends. Nothing would get broken."

Ewan smiled. "You're beautiful and you're lying next to me."

He reached out to her and I entered his arms. I can only be what I was born to be.

Trust me, I wanted things to go back to the way they were, free and easy, but Ada couldn't do it. It was too late, now that she loved him. She started feeling guilty all the time, imagining how it would feel for his girlfriend if she knew about their affair. It was easy to imagine the pain of betrayal—after all, Ada loved him too now. She and the girl were basically on the same side. He and I were, for all purposes, the villains in this.

Also, Ada had gotten the Depo-Provera shot, a load of hormones that made her bleed for eight weeks nonstop. It threw off the fragile balance she and I kept in her mind, and there were terrible mood swings, a gutting depression. Ada owned a bokken, a wooden Japanese sword, and one night she used it to smash the mirror in her dorm room, screaming tears as glass flew across the hardwood floor. The shards glinted in her fingers as she drew them down the inside of her arm, watching the bright red bubble through brown skin. I moaned inside her, greedy for the mother color she was feeding me. We were pulling apart. Ada sat on the floor surrounded by a hundred mirror pieces and cried.

Her friend Catia, a military brat who hung out with her and Malena, came by to get Ada for lunch. She saw the mess and the blood and sighed.

"Oh, Ada," she said. "Let's clean this up."

I liked her for that, for how she never made Ada feel damaged. Ada loved her. Catia was quiet but forceful, a pastor's daughter. On a night run to Taco Bell once, when Catia was driving and Malena was sitting in the back with Ada, they stopped at a liquor store and Malena bought her usual bottle of Johnnie Walker, tipping some of it to the ground before getting back in the car. She offered some to Ada, but Ada refused. Now that she drank, I preferred her to stick to tequila. Malena looked at Ada and knew she was thinking about Ewan.

"He loves you, Ada. He just doesn't know it yet."

Ada made a face. "Yeah, whatever," she said.

Malena shrugged with half-lidded eyes. "You'll see, mi hermana. You'll see."

Catia smiled slightly at us through the rearview mirror, and Ada looked out the window, her heart hurting. Ewan had started cleaning up his life after a bad Salvia trip he had one night, when he said Ada came to him in a vision, sent by the devil. He said it was her, but if there was anyone a devil would send, we all know by now—it would be me. Ewan just couldn't tell the difference.

"Clearly, we're both way too Catholic," I joked, but he was serious. He stopped smoking weed; he cut back on the drinking and focused on his classes. Ada was so proud of him. I was alarmed.

"I've given up all my vices," he said. "Except you."

"You're going to give me up?" Ada whispered. I could taste the grief in the back of her throat. She didn't want to be just another drug polluting his life, and she wasn't, she really wasn't. It was me, but we were one, so I didn't know what to tell her.

Ewan looked at her sadly. "I don't know if I can," he admitted.

The whole thing became a loop, as these things often do. Ada stopped sleeping with Ewan, so I stopped fucking him, and instead they cooked together at his new place, making nasi goreng in a smooth dance across the kitchen floor, with knife and cutting board, onions and meat, oil and spices. He tossed the wok and washed the dishes, and Ada was so happy. I left her alone that night—it had been so long since she could be this happy. She made him watch *Sarafina!* and they ate Cadbury chocolates and fell asleep and nothing happened. But then, eventually, I fell back into bed with him and the cycle started again and the guilt was everywhere, greasy and thick, and Ada couldn't get away.

Eventually, Ewan was the one who ended it.

"I can't do this anymore," he said. "I can't be with you anymore. She makes me happy."

For the first time, I let Ada cry in front of him. I watched her sob into his shoulder, into the soft cotton of his T-shirt. She didn't beg him; she didn't ask for anything. Ewan held her and touched her face gently.

"Why do you have to be so beautiful?" he whispered.

Ada cried herself to sleep, her face pressed into his chest. She woke up briefly to see Ewan watching her sleep, his hand playing in the curls of her hair, his eyes soft.

Ada graduated college a few weeks later with Catia and Malena and Luka and most of her friends. Saachi flew up for it with Añuli and Chima, and the whole time, Ada was unsettled and shaking. I had to keep her face smooth so that her human family wouldn't see any of the storm within. Saachi was demanding her time, too much of it, considering that Ada was about to lose all her friends and there was barely any time to say good-bye.

"We came all the way here," Saachi told her. "The least you can do is spend time with us."

None of it fucking mattered, honestly. Ada and I had lost Ewan. Since the night he'd rejected us, I'd slept with him once, a final time before Ada's graduation. He and I were in her room, on the raised bed, moonlight spitting through the glass of her window. Ewan was drunk and high, back from a night of bad decisions that ended, as usual, with him looking for Ada and fucking me. He wrenched her hair until her neck and spine cracked loudly, and when we were face to face, I found myself opening Ada's mouth and saying the same words Soren once told her.

"I fucking love you," I said.

Ewan kept thrusting, pounding in the dark, and when he spoke, his voice was a stranger's, slurred and hard.

"Shut the fuck up," he said.

I swear, I never felt more stupid and useless than I did in that moment; like I was some whore he was just dumping into. Ada knew how Ewan was when he was drunk and high, when he pissed on coffee tables, when he couldn't remember a thing that he'd done or said—which was the case this time. He went back to himself in the days afterward, but it didn't matter. He had already insulted me, and wallahi, I was unforgiving and petty and vindictive. Don't expect anything else from an ọgbanje.

I targeted one of Ewan's friends on the tennis team, a boy who had always seemed to hate Ada, but I could see him and I could smell the truth. Ada was a beautiful girl and this friend had to watch her, knowing that Ewan got to fuck her and he didn't. He was human. There was bound to be desire lying under his hatred—there always is. So it was easy to take him home at the end of one night, and of course he agreed. He kissed me and sank his fingers into Ada's body before coming with my hand wrapped around him. I kicked him out of Ada's room as soon as we were done and turned inward.

"Really?" said Ada. She was folding her arms and leaning against the marble, her eyes red from crying over Ewan. "His friend?"

"And so?" I answered. "Ewan won't care. He let us go, remember? He doesn't love us. He made that fucking clear."

Ada winced and looked away. I came close to her and ran my hand along her cheek.

"Don't worry," I whispered. "Fine girl. There are others who will want us, who I can make want us. It's easy."

I had her put her pain with me because I could use it as fuel, I could do things with it that she couldn't. Like fucking one of the track runners, a boy with a silken Southern drawl and hooded eyes that dripped sex from the lashes. Trust me, I didn't need Ewan, and if Ada thought she did, I would make her forget. There were many, many other things we could be doing.

Saachi and Chima were angry because Ada insisted on flying to Georgia to spend a month with her friend Itohan, instead of coming straight to Saachi's house with them. I didn't give a shit about their anger—mine was much larger and stronger. Except for Añuli, they'd soured the graduation for Ada, keeping her from her friends, the people who really knew what was going on in her life. She didn't know when she'd see Malena or Catia again. Luka was going back to Serbia. Axel and Denis were going to Iceland to coach volleyball, Juan was going back to Mexico. The house at the bottom of the hill was going to be empty.

We had lost Ewan. Ada was devastated, but I had work to do, so we went to Georgia.

It felt strange to be back there. Things there were the same, but everything for Ada and I was completely different because we'd just spent a whole year with Ewan. I was done with him. I wanted him out of Ada's head and I wanted her to stop loving him. I was furious. I wanted a new toy and I already knew I was going to play rough. It's not as if there was gentleness in me to start with. I was hungry and I was hunting. I couldn't stop myself and I didn't want to—the whole point of my existence was to run wild and tear whoever fell into my mouth into pieces. I picked Itohan's other brother, the older one. I started grooming him, which was easy because he and Ada were close, and after about a week or two of this, Itohan pulled Ada aside, saying they needed to talk.

"What's up?" Ada asked, her face open and friendly. I lurked behind it, as usual.

"I know you don't know how it looks," Itohan said, her long hair roughly pushed behind an ear, her lipstick matte and red. "When you and him are hanging out upstairs and the rest of us are downstairs."

"He was just showing me his books," Ada said, and I fought to keep from laughing out of her mouth.

"I know." Itohan kept her voice friendly. "But it's just somehow when you and him are alone in his room together."

She smiled, trying to be kind. Inside the marble room, I let out a shriek of laughter and Ada kicked me in the shin, hissing at me to shut up. On her face, she was maintaining a worried and slightly scared frown for Itohan's benefit.

"I know it's not intentional," Itohan was saying, "but just think about how it looks, okay? You two can't date, not after you dated my younger brother."

The marble suddenly felt cold around me. "Wow," I said, my laughter fading. "She really thinks we don't know what we're doing."

"Good," muttered Ada. "Lucky for me."

I couldn't fucking believe it. They still saw only Ada; they still gave her the benefit of the doubt even when you'd have to be an idiot not to realize how it looked, as Itohan put it. It was amazing. I had planned every touch of skin, every coy glance that wove the older brother in, yet everyone stayed blind. It was as if they were all stuck in that nice, innocent Christian world Ada used to be a part of, before she was ripped out by my birth. And now, after everything that had happened with Ewan, there was absolutely no way Ada could return. She was an imposter; she was now me. I'd contaminated her too much—we had done too much together.

So she and I nodded obediently at Itohan, but I had no intention of stopping. What for? I wasn't finished with the older brother, not yet. I had spent weeks trying to crack him open the way I wanted. I played soft and sweet, I pretended to be Ada since she was the one he loved. I brushed her fingertips over the back of his hand as he drove and gave him shy smiles till we were alone, and then I slid my palms over his jeans, but he stopped me. Maybe he could smell the difference between her and me, between the grassy lemon of her and my coppered scent. I don't know what it was—maybe he just knew her well enough to know who I wasn't. But he wouldn't surrender and it made me angry. I told him I loved him and he still wouldn't surrender, he wouldn't let me touch him. I had arrived in Georgia wrapped in a red rage, and after Ewan, this second refusal blinded me with fury. He denied me at his own risk.

So the night before Ada was leaving, I slid her out of the guest room and into the younger brother's room. He was the type I knew, easy and predictable. I fucked him with Ada's body, with his older brother in the next room, asleep and still in love with Ada, with their mother down the hall next to her Bible. The next morning, I sat the older brother down and pretended to be Ada and told him that she had never loved him, a trick I learned from Soren. I watched his heart crack and fall into shimmering pieces of dust, and it was good, it felt correct. This was the lesson: I can fuck you or I can fuck you up—simple.

After I hurt him, he still got up and drove Ada to the airport. You see, what I realized later was that he wasn't like the others I targeted. He was gentle; he didn't deserve to be punished. But we had lost Ewan and I was there and I was born into what I was born into. I have always been a weapon and I am not obliged to be fair. My only mistake was that I forgot one small detail: Ada did love the older brother. Very much, in fact.

I didn't know it at the time, but I had gone too far.

Chapter Eleven

You will always be in the process of change because every time you get born into a basilisk, that basilisk consumes itself so you can be born into another basilisk.

We

Asụghara could not be left alone; that would be unnatural. When something stands, something else stands beside it. So on the day she was born in Virginia, there was another one born with her as she tore through that window. His name was Saint Vincent, because when he sloughed off Asụghara's side, he fell with holiness on his hands.

The Ada named him and he remained in the marble of her mind because he couldn't survive her body. Saint Vincent was long fingered and cool, with slow and simmering hungers. He was strange; we could never quite place him, where his parts came from. He was not expected to come through the window, but he did and so he was born in a portal, a son of flux space.

What we mean is that he was not godspawn like Asụghara. He belonged nowhere, except maybe to the Ada. He was gentle, soft as a ghost. That was good—he was no threat to Asụghara, he would not compete with her for control.

No, Saint Vincent preferred to move inside the Ada's dreams, when she was floating in our realm, untethered and malleable. He molded her into a new body there, a dreambody with reorganized flesh and a penis complete with functioning nerves and expanding blood vessels, tautening easily into an erection. Even Asụghara was impressed; she couldn't mold or build in our realm the way that he could. Saint Vincent used the dreambody as his. He wove other bodies in our realm for him to ride, for him to place astride his hips, swallowing him up. When he came, his pleasure was a concentrated burst of light, anchored and distilled in his groin. It was different from what Asụghara experienced with the Ada's body—those orgasms would spread in a diffuse wash that drowned her. This separation of pleasures was good: Saint Vincent stayed in our realm and in the marble of the Ada's mind, while Asụghara met him in the marble but moved in the flesh.

He was no less holy for the things he did with the dreambody—you must understand that we see holy as removed from flesh and therefore purer. Saint Vincent was uncontaminated, quarantined, even. Perhaps in another world, where the Ada was not split and segmented, she and Saint Vincent might have been one thing together. After all, she was always being mistaken for a boy when she was a child, when her hair was short for the first time. Perhaps he had been there all along and we just never noticed, we were so young.

The Ada had liked being seen as a boy. She felt like it fit, or at least the misfit of it fit, the wrongness was right. She was perhaps eleven years old then. Her chest was flat, her hips were narrow, her hair was short, and there must have been something about her face that wasn't delicate enough. When she went swimming at the local sports club with Lisa, adults would stop her in the women's changing room.

"Why are you in here?" they'd ask, or, "Why are you wearing a girl's swimsuit?"

The Ada felt like a trickster, which felt right. She could move between boy and girl, which was a freedom, for her and for us. But when she turned twelve and started bleeding, everything was ruined. The hormones redid her body, remaking it without consent from us or the Ada. We were distressed at this re-forming of our vessel, very much so, because it was nothing other than a cruel reminder that we were now flesh, that we could not control our form, that we were in a cage that obeyed other laws, human laws. We had no choice in this warping, this unnatural maturing. There was blackish blood, a swelling chest, hair sprouting like an evil forest. It pushed us into a space we hated, a marked plane that was too clear and too wrong.

Around that time, one afternoon, the Ada was walking down the road with her cousin Obiageli. The Ada said something rude, a touch insolent, and Obiageli reacted by reaching out and poking her finger into the Ada's chest, right in her new breasts.

"Because you have these apples now, ehn? That's why you're talking like that?" Obiageli chuckled at the Ada's shocked face and kept walking.

Inside the Ada, we shuddered and retched from that touch, turning her stomach over. The quick revulsion wouldn't go away. We were loud and kicking against this meatbody we'd been shoved into; we wanted to be let out, this was an abomination. But the Ada had learned her trick of quick sacrifices just that year, so when they got back to the house, she cut into the back of her hand and bled us into a restless silence. She would continue, if you remember, for another twelve years, but back then was when she learned that the sacrifices worked, that using blood could make existence bearable, at least for a little while.

She tried to make us comfortable, as if in apology for her bleeding and bulging body; she dug into Saul's old suitcases and found his shirts from when he lived in London, button-downs that were too big for her, which was perfect. The Ada covered her new body in flowered red polyester and crisp green cotton, hiding it away. She wore loose cargo trousers in army green with seven deep pockets, until the cuffs tore and frayed. When she overheard one of her classmates describe her as busty, she decided it was not real. It felt like he was talking about someone else.

All of this is to say that everything has existed in another form prior to its current one, so when Saint Vincent showed up, the Ada was not surprised. She welcomed his delicate masculinity arranging itself in folds inside her; she welcomed his company because she was, of course, always lonely. It brought her a small amount of grief when she realized that he was restricted to using only a dreambody because hers was simply wrong. Her body worked for Asụghara, but Saint Vincent would be neutered within it, with nothing weighing down between his legs, just canals lined in velveteen. His hungers were different, but simple. Saint Vincent wanted the soft nape of a girl's neck against his mouth and he wanted it enough that the Ada went to get it for him.

It was a clumsy attempt. The Ada tried to explain the existence of Saint Vincent to one of her college friends who he found beautiful, but this was the Ada and she was not Asụghara, she did not have that silken charm. So the conversation was awkward, and as the Ada spoke the words exposing Saint Vincent's existence and desires, she knew it sounded crazy; you could not put him into a mouth and expect it to sound sane. Her beautiful friend was polite but uninterested, and she turned the Ada down. It should not have been surprising, yet the Ada found herself retreating inside her mind, humiliated by this rejection, confused and hurt.

"Stupid, stupid, stupid," she muttered to herself as she paced around the marble. "Of course she doesn't want you. Who would?"

"It's enough." Asụghara stepped in and grabbed the Ada's arms, pinning them at her sides, leaning her forehead against the Ada's. "You tried. It's enough. We won't tell anyone about him ever again, you hear? We'll keep him in here. No one except us can understand."

Teary-eyed, the Ada nodded, and just like that, Saint Vincent became a secret buried in the marble. Perhaps it is not how we would have done things, but as we said, the beastself was running things and she thought it was for the best. It was how she moved; she pushed them back and hid them in the marble in order to protect them—first the Ada, and now Saint Vincent. Asụghara was the blade, forever flirting with the softness of people's throats. They were balanced now—the Ada, her little beast, and her saint—the three of them locked in marbled flesh, burning through the world.

But no matter what skins they shed in this foreign country, we remembered where they came from and we remembered the first mother. Ala is all earth, no matter the oceans; the Ada was still walking on soil that belonged to her mother. Even her flesh belonged to Ala, for, as we have said, it is on her lips that humans are born, and there they live until they die. We were still her children, distilled into tripled hatchlings. Otu nne na-amụ, mana ọ bụghị otu chi na-eke. And to be named is to gain power, let alone to be named thrice over. Our heat was building, spilling through the gates, calling the others, pulling them like a sun with weight. We should have known, we should have been warned—the children of our mother do not forget pacts and their oaths taste of anger and alligator pepper. They were gathering in rain clouds, their voices distant and dreamlike, but grating like torn metal.

You are looking for our trouble, they sang. Gin spilled on the soil, blood wiped over clay, and they spoke in a legion of voices.

What are you going to do when we come?

Chapter Twelve

I can die today, I can die tomorrow.

Asụghara

I heard the clacking first.

It was rhythmic and regular, bouncing off the walls and domed ceilings of Ada's mind. "Stop it, Vincent," I said, not turning around. "I don't like that sound." Sometimes he got restless and did things that irritated the hell out of me, like whistling ghost-birds across the ceiling or turning the marble into a maze of crying walls. I wasn't in the mood for another of his games. I had been having a quiet morning standing at Ada's eyes, not really doing anything, just looking out into her world.

The clacking continued, and under it I could hear a soft brushing that made my bones start to itch. That was definitely not Vincent. I turned around with my fingernails biting into my palms and I saw the first one. It was moving across the floor toward me, wearing a hooded bodysuit woven from twisted raffia that had been dyed red and black and fringed with grass at the wrists and ankles. It was clacking with its carved teeth, low to the floor, sweeping its legs out in wide circles.

I took a step back. "Who the fuck are you?"

The thing laughed, like rattling fingers. *Eh henh,* it said. *We knew you would forget, nwanne anyị.*

The hair on the back of my neck went taut and electric. I knew that voice from somewhere. The thing stopped moving and unfolded itself upright. A hole opened in its chest. Xylophone music hammered out and the second thing tumbled forward from inside it. This one looked like a young girl, short hair stained with camwood, skin dusted with nzu, coral slings over the chest. It sprang up and laughed at me.

See your face, it said. *Were you not expecting us? After you went and became just one, by yourself!* It danced a short burst to the xylophone music still spilling from the first one.

Oh, I realized, of course. I should have recognized them—the brothersisters, children of our first mother, ndị otu. A spike of exhilaration shot up through me and I laughed. These were the mischief-makers, you see, the tricksters; they were like me. They didn't give a shit about humans, they enjoyed causing pain—they were me and I was them. It was the best visit I'd ever had in the marble, a thousand times better than having Yshwa show up with his sanctimonious nonsense.

The first one scratched the raised black spots on the sides of its mask-face, slowly rotating its head all the way around like an owl, following me as I walked around them.

"Okay," I said. "No wahala. So it's now you decided to come?"

Come, come and see, come and see you, little animal. The second one had a lighter voice, like thin metal. *Little evil of the forest.*

The first one was chains dragging on broken shells. *Yes o, come and see you, see if you know who your people are.*

Who you belong to, chimed the second one.

The first nodded. *What you smell like.*

I stopped walking. "And what do I smell like?" I asked.

The second brothersister curled its mouth up till the lips almost touched its nose.

Like flesh, it spat. *Bad flesh.*

That annoyed me. "I didn't ask to be put here," I pointed out.

'*I didn't ask to be put here,*' mocked the first. *And what are you doing about it? It's like you like it.*

We don't like it, said the second. *Who told you to come here?*

The first answer that came to mind was Ada. That she was the one who called me and I came for her. Instead, I shrugged. "I already told you, I didn't ask for it."

Who told you to stay here? You don't know road again?

"Road to where?"

The second one shook its head and turned away, hissing. The first one sighed and lunged toward me, flicking the grass cuff of its wrist on my face. *It's like you went and forgot everything,* it said.

Its touch was like a machete running me through. I wrapped my arms around my stomach, shocked. Pain was not a feeling I was familiar with—that was Ada's thing, not mine. Everything around us slowed down. I could see dust lightly sifting through the air, settling on the marble and the creases of my skin. The two of them smelled strange, like hope, like something fucking with the fine edges of my memory, something I was hungry for but couldn't remember the taste of. It hurt. I felt tears fill my eyes and I doubled up, trying to fight it. I didn't want to cry in front of them. The second one turned back to me and reached out its arm, holding a sheaf of young palm fronds. It brushed the bruisable green against my skin, from my forehead to my chin, and smiled, its teeth filed sharp.

Yes, it said softly. *It pains like that. Imagine how the rest of us feel, twenty-times-twenty times worse than that, since you went, since you did not come back. Imagine, watching you stay on this side, away from us, watching you and watching you, and now you smell different, so we said, 'Let us come.'*

Still bad flesh, marked the first. *But different.*

The second brushed my face again and I closed my eyes. *Do you know who your people are?*

The first leaned forward with its mouth full of shards. *Are you remembering yet?*

My skin readjusted slightly. "I never forgot," I whispered, and somehow, I wasn't lying.

Eziokwu? It dragged its voice sarcastically. *Who are your people?*

Goose bumps rippled over my skin. "You," I said.

Is that so? They were testing, teasing.

I opened my eyes and put some irritation into my voice. "Who else?"

They spun in small, precise circles.

Ask us, they said. It was rhetorical. *Maybe you think the small girl and those humans are your people.*

I thought about it. I had come for Ada. I had stayed for Ada. I loved her and they knew I loved her. Still, I shook my head. "No, I don't belong. I know I don't belong."

They clucked in mock pity and the first one ran its grass cuff under my chin. It tickled and I moved my face away. The second one squatted and its coral slings drummed against each other.

Are you not hungry to go home?

The machete twisted as they said that, opening a cave inside me. I felt like I was starving, being eaten up by myself. I couldn't tell if it was real or them.

"Yes," I choked out. The dust in the air seemed to shine. My knees softened and they helped me to the floor. My weakness terrified me. I held so much power in Ada's world, you see, but in here, with them, I could feel their age press on me. They were older than even Yshwa, old as forever, born of the first mother. Here, with them, I bent.

Do you remember the pact?

Their faces were like skies above me. I felt the marble on the back of my skull and shook my head. All I could remember was bits of red dust and masks, fragments of that first day when we, the larger of me, started to wake up. The gold pins I had been wearing in my hair crawled away, spreading curls over the floor like a black stain. It was becoming hard to think—they had muddied the air; they had slowed my mouth and blood.

She doesn't remember anything, the second one sang to the first. *She's been wiped clean.*

She doesn't remember the basking, the twenty days, agreed the first.

"What twenty days?" I asked. My head was swimming.

After our mother shed, twenty days, and then we were laid.

The second one laid its body down next to me, coral swooping to the floor. *Encased in soft white, veins forming first,* it said. *You don't remember. This is your hatching story.*

In the heat, the first one added as it hooked its hands under my armpits, dragging me to my feet. *Ngwa, stand up and remember.*

I staggered and tried to clear my head. The smaller second one looked up at me, its face pensive.

We lay against each other before we were even whole, it said. It floated up as though pushed by a breeze and swayed, closing its eyes.

The first one pulled its grass-fringed hands from my body, leaving me standing there like a lost tree.

Touch her, it said. *Let her know again.*

The second one danced forward on its toes, stretched its white-dusted finger and pressed it to the center of my chest. My sternum collapsed and turned me inside out, and suddenly I was somewhere dark. I could see nothing, yet an overwhelming presence was around me. It felt like millions of eyes looking at me, like I was stripped down and I couldn't see anyone who could see me, like they were eating me up and my mouth was gagged. I started panicking, my face sealed shut, I couldn't even flail the way I wanted to, and then I was back in the marble, gasping, leaning against the twisted raffia of the first one. It smelled like smoke and palm wine.

I stumbled away from it, retching. "What the fuck did you do? What happened?"

They seemed undisturbed. *It has been a very long time since you were back with us. The list against you continues to grow.*

Nke mbu, you crossed over and broke your gates.

"It wasn't me," I said. "I don't know what happened."

If you don't know what happened, how do you know it wasn't you?

You always like to blame someone else.

"You're seriously trying to blame the gates on me?" I wanted to hear them accuse me directly, but they evaded.

Are they not your gates?

"I didn't fucking break them! You think I wanted to end up like this?"

Somebody broke them. You're the one who passed through.

I hissed at them. "That just means you don't know who fucked up the gates. I'm not going to take responsibility for something I didn't do. Forget that nonsense."

They smelled irritated. Spots were dancing in my eyes.

The second thing is that you didn't come back immediately.

"How was I supposed to do that? I'm only one, in case you forgot. I wasn't even there."

You were there. The bigger you. You can tell the rest of them for us.

The third thing is that you crossed an ocean and you went far away and you didn't listen to us.

No, the fourth thing is that you didn't listen to us.

I pressed my hands to my head. "Chineke. You've been holding these grudges all this time? That's what you came here for?"

The first brothersister scratched its spots again and swiveled its neck. The second one tapped out a pattern with its heels on the marble and it echoed. The dust stopped moving.

Look, said the second one eventually. *We can leave you, nsogbu adịghị, but we are not the only ones.*

The first one scoffed. *We are not even the angry ones.*

My dizziness was leaving. I shook off the rest of it and glared at them. "Tell me why you really came here," I said.

They looked at each other, then turned to me, moving like twins.

Come back, they said. *Listen to us this time.* They pressed on either side of me and pulled me over, back to their memories of the other side beyond the gates, of what used to be mine too, the solid comfort, the thousand-souled other brothersisters all folded against each other, never alone, as alone as you could want to be—anything, everything we ever wanted, even nothingness, if we chose that, even ends. I started crying at the freedom of it all, at what they had given back to me—these memories of a time before the shell-blue walls in Umuahia. When they stepped away, I fell to the floor.

I was still lying on the veined marble when they started to disappear, their voices grating against each other.

Come back.

There is still time. The Obi may kneel down, but it never crumbles.

The way up is the way down. This is your last warning.

I kept crying for a while after they were gone, until I got tired of it and stopped. The marble had warmed up and I could almost feel Ada's pulse through it. It was strange—I thought that I would feel drained but it was the opposite. I felt full of a rich and thick power. It tasted like if you roasted blood with salt and capped it in a jar, cooked with it, seasoned meat with it, fed it to your lovers rare, red on trembling fingers. I suppose that's what having your memories back will do to you. I was still trapped here, I knew that, but I was not empty-handed. To have a body to work with is no joke. I had all this room under Ada's warm and nervous skin, and not only that, but I had all her bones too, hinged together, down to the marrow. Even there, I had the marrowspace, those little air pockets between the secret flesh, the flesh inside the enamel.

I had been playing with Ada all this time, just little games, but even those can be done with much power. After all, was I not the hunger in Ada? I was made out of desire, I tasted of it, I filled her up with it and choked her, lying over her like a killing cloud, soft and unstoppable, all the weight of a wet sky. My power was so absolute that she couldn't tell where she was and it didn't matter—it was a reminder that I was there. I wanted her to know me well and never feel alone, to always remember that no one could fuck her up as well as me, no one could get her as high as I could. Ada could pretend as if she hated me, but you can't hide the truth. I felt how tightly she held me, how she didn't want to come down or let me go, how she didn't care about the cold or the pain because she had me, and wallahi, I was better than drugs, better than alcohol; she was never sober with me. I was the best high, the fastest, most reliable dealer, the best beast. Why would Ada ever want to wake up from me? Even when she couldn't cut her skin anymore, I was sharp enough to do it from the inside because we both knew the sacrifices could never stop.

After the brothersisters visited me, my purpose became clear. My existence was offering Ada a temporary solution, you see, but they'd reminded me that there was another option, and the best part was that I could do both things—I could honor the oath while protecting Ada. It was perfect. She was me and I was her, so by returning to the other side, I would be taking her away from this useless human realm, and what better protection could I offer her, really? I had done what I could so far, with the boys and the drinking and the fucking, but I could do better. I could be better. I could change Ada's world. We could all go home.

ỊLAGHACHỊ

(To Return)

Chapter Thirteen

Do not hang your heart on me.

Asụghara

We had settled into a rhythm by now. Even though Ada named us, I think she was surprised at how quickly Saint Vincent and I took on these names, how distinct we became. She wasn't sure if we were real, but nothing about us felt false. I told her to keep us inside her head, in the marble room, so that no one could see us. They would've told Ada that she was crazy or that we weren't real, and I couldn't allow those lies. I had to protect us. When I made Ada do things she didn't want to, I wasn't doing it to be cruel. The whole is greater than the individual.

So when she started looking up her "symptoms," it felt like a betrayal—like she thought we were abnormal. How can, when we were her and she was us? I watched her try to tell people about us and I smiled when they told her that it was normal to have different parts of yourself. "You're just like everyone else," they said, because they were just like everyone else; like Itohan's family, they couldn't see the kind of thing Ada had become.

"It's fine," I said to a worried Vincent. "Let her play this stupid game." Eventually Ada would realize what I'd been telling her: she didn't need people to understand; she only needed us. I let her read up on personality disorders, and once in a while, I'd tell her to stop looking, even though I knew she wouldn't listen.

Ada wanted a reason, a better explanation. We were not enough. We were too strange. She had been raised by humans, medical ones at that. So instead she read lists of diagnostic criteria, things like disruption of identity, self-damaging impulsivity, emotional instability and mood swings, self-mutilating behavior and recurrent suicidal behavior. I could have told her it was all me, even that last one. Especially that last one. Maybe all her research was done in self-preservation, because she didn't trust me to save her. I wanted her to die, yes, but like I said before, everything I did was in our best interests. I was just trying to save her.

And for the record, she was the one who tried to kill me first.

It's fine if I seem selfish, running through the world with a body that didn't really belong to me. But I was considerate, even when I didn't have to be. Take, for instance, the kind of men I allowed to touch Ada's body. Some of them wanted Ada, not me, so I removed them because it was impossible—in those sweaty moments, there was only me. The gentle ones were useless. They would touch Ada's body as if she was made of spun sugar, brittle like Saachi's teeth, stretched like Saul's temper. Let me tell you the truth about men like that—they want soft moons. They want women with just enough crescent to provide a sufficient edge, tender little slivers of light that they can bring home to their mothers. Like I said, useless. I didn't want them near me. After what happened with Itohan's older brother, I had learned what I could do to men like that, and it was better for them to just lock their doors against me, because I was coming over the hill like a monster.

I allowed myself to love Ewan, even though he was human, because I thought, well, this one can handle me. He is a liar and a cheat after all, he even deserves me. But after he walked away, and after Itohan's brothers, I only hunted cruel men, men who also cheated and lied, who broke things with the selfishness of their hands. They were violent in bed—they knew how to fuck me as if I was made of rage and metal. It felt as if they could seize the sky and force it to its knees. I wanted to lock myself in with them and run out of air, to be loved like the weapon I was, to lie in bruises like a monster.

In retrospect, it is not surprising that Ada tried to kill me then. I had dragged her through unprecedented filth in the name of protection.

"I don't know what it'll take," she told me, when we were both standing in the marble room. "Therapy, probably. But I can't do this anymore. I need you gone."

I was manifesting strongly that day, wearing her face, but with sharper cheekbones and fuller lips. Saint Vincent watched us with his eyelids drooping.

Ada twisted her hands. "I'm trying to do what's best for me," she said.

"What do you think I've been doing this whole time?" I snapped. "What do you think I was doing when I came through Soren's window in the first place?" I watched as she winced and looked away. "You see? It's like you're forgetting I'm the only one who protected you."

"I'm trying to protect myself now," she said, and I did a double take.

"From who?" I was starting to see red, the mother color crawling over my eyes. "From me? You want to protect yourself from me?" I didn't realize I had stepped forward until she backed away. Vincent sat up, purple shadows under his eyes.

"Asụghara, she didn't mean it like that."

I took another step until my mouth was by Ada's ear. I was taller than her, stronger than her. "Of course not. How can? When I've been the one holding her together? She can't have meant it like that. She would have to be mad to say something that fucking stupid."

Ada's eyes were filling with angry tears. "I'm not stupid," she bit out, and she sounded like a child filled with hurt.

I cupped her face in my hand and my fingernails were golden against her skin.

"Of course not," I said, softening my voice. "But you're not a fighter, Ada. All these men just want to fuck you, and it's my job to be there. Allow me to be strong for you." I leaned my forehead against hers, but Ada pulled away.

"You weren't strong enough to ever say no," she said, and if she had said it gently, it would have been one thing, but she said it with cruelty and she sounded like me. I stepped back and tasted fresh anger inside my mouth.

"Fuck you," I said. "You know who I am, you know what I have to do. I don't have a choice."

"Are you mad? I'm the one without a choice!" Ada shoved me and I staggered back. "Not you, me! You're just selfish!"

"Me, selfish? I'm doing all of this for *you*."

"Oh my god." Ada put her hands over her face and paced around the marble. "You don't do it for me, Asụghara, you do it because you like it."

I stared at her. "What?"

"I was there too, remember? Itohan's older brother?" She turned back to face me. "You enjoyed hurting him, even though he didn't do anything to us. You thought it was funny."

I looked at the contempt on her face and felt myself calming. What was I doing, begging a human not to banish me from flesh? As if she could even do it. I walked away and sat down next to Vincent, then I tried to reason with the girl.

"Everything we do is a weapon, Ada, you get it? You think no one has ever seen our pain and laughed before? Don't be ridiculous. They do it to us, we do it to them. Simple."

Saint Vincent loosened the collar of his shirt and lit a cigarette. He smelled like Ewan. Ada leaned against the wall and folded her arms.

"I don't need to do that anymore," she said. "I don't need you anymore."

"Is that so?" I narrowed my eyes against the smoke from Vincent's mouth. "Who will you need now? Yshwa, the one who gives you nothing?"

Ada glared at me and I took the cigarette from Vincent. He walked over to her, pulling her into his arms.

"Asụghara loves you," he said, as if I couldn't hear him. "She just doesn't want to leave you alone."

I threw my middle finger up at them and blew a veil of smoke in front of my face. Ada shook her head at me.

"You're hurting people I love, don't you understand?" she said. "I can't just fold my hands and watch you do it."

"You're doing this for them?" I put out the cigarette. Maybe she didn't understand. "They deserved it, Ada. All of them deserved it for what we went through."

"Come on, that's not true," she said. "Even the ones who didn't have anything to do with it? Even the innocent ones?"

When I heard her say that, something broke inside me.

"Were we *not innocent?"* I shouted, my voice slamming against the marble and splintering it. Cracks ran through the

walls and ceiling, and Ada and Vincent froze where they were standing. All I could see was the mother color. "Were *we* not innocent enough to be spared?!"

They continued staring at me.

"No? Okay then, so tell me, *why should I spare them?*"

The room fell silent and I saw Vincent's tears first, but I didn't realize I was crying until Ada came up to me and wiped my face gently. "I didn't realize. I'm so sorry," she whispered, as if she wasn't the victim. "I'm so sorry they hurt you too."

I didn't want her pity. "I'm not going anywhere," I told her, pulling away from her hands. What could she do? I was stronger than her; this marble was my realm more than it was hers. So I made myself bigger and bigger, and she was saying something but her voice was small and tiny, and I was pressed up against the walls of her mind, growing and growing until she was a dot in a corner and I couldn't hear her voice anymore.

Look, I was a hungry shade, nothing more. I latched onto the men, and their energy felt like sticky fruit sliding between my fingers, and when we were done, I was still hungry. And after the next time, I was still hungry. And after the one after that one, I was still hungry. I would have drowned them all. I would have inched slowly over their bodies, dipped my fingers inside their throats and ripped out sounds. I filled their beds with secrets. Ada was right—I found pleasure in evil. I did many things in hunger that could be misconstrued.

Chapter Fourteen

Ebe onye dara, ka chi ya kwatụrụ ya.

Asụghara

As far as I'm concerned, I have been loyal, both to Ada and the brothersisters. When Ada tried to look for help, I did many things to stop it because she was mine, but believe me, I never wanted her to feel alone. After she tried to kill me and failed, Ada gave up. I didn't enjoy winning that fight. There's no delight in watching her crumble—that's only fun when it happens to other people. Saint Vincent and I tried to make a home for Ada in her mind, and that meant something, at least to me. You don't know what it's like to share a life and a body, to watch the days and months and years drag by, the people who came in and revolved out, to watch Ada try and get away from us, to see her fail, to see the way she came to love us better, eventually.

I even finally allowed Ada to see her therapists, since she was being so stubborn about it. I remember one session with a middle-aged woman who had gray streaks in her hair. Ada was sitting there, rubbing the back of her left hand with her right one, tracing the tendon that led to her middle finger, running her fingertips lightly over it until she felt it roll under and across. This was something she did often, just to remind herself that she had a physical body. She was also talking to herself in her head, and I could hear the forced calm that she was injecting into her voice.

"It's okay, baby, you're fine. It's only an hour, then we can go. We're fine, baby, it's okay."

The woman with the streaked hair was talking, but Ada had stopped listening. I looked around the office, wondering how many times we'd been here. I didn't always follow what Ada had been up to, so things easily slipped by me when I wasn't paying attention.

"Do you have any questions?" the woman asked. "Comments? Concerns?"

"None," said Ada.

The therapist made a note, her pen scratching quietly. "How do you feel about your future?" she asked.

Without thinking, Ada let the truth slip out. "Indifferent."

The therapist's face sharpened. "Could you elaborate on that a bit more? When you think about the future, exactly what emotions come up for you?"

Ada shrugged. "Indifference."

The therapist continued pushing, and as she spoke, Ada kept blanking out midway through the woman's sentences, then returning. The therapist asked the same things over and over, rephrasing them as if Ada wouldn't notice. But it didn't matter how many ways she twisted the questions, Ada had no answers.

"What about Asụghara?" the woman asked, and suddenly I was paying all the attention I had in the world.

"How the fuck does she know my name?" I hissed at Ada, but she ignored me.

"Are there any more of them?" continued the therapist, and I watched Ada with my breath held. I could tell that she didn't want to lie. She'd already lied once, when the woman asked what the suicide plan was, which even Ada knew was a truly stupid question. Why would anyone give away a suicide plan—so it could be stopped? What nonsense.

But I could see that Ada was actually considering telling this woman, this complete fucking stranger, about Saint Vincent. I reached out across all the marble and pushed a thousand spikes into it. The pain would reach Ada, whether she tried to ignore me or not.

"We don't talk about Vincent," I reminded her. "Better keep your fucking mouth shut."

"I'm not comfortable discussing that," Ada answered obediently, and the therapist let it go.

For the rest of the session, Ada drew imaginary lines on her temple, pressing her index finger into the skin, the pressure holding her together. She traced her eyebrows and tried to find words to tell the therapist about the things I had done to her mind. But I choked up the words and made them rot in her throat—there would be no screaming for help.

When Ada finally left the office, I waited until her feet hit the stone steps outside before I started shouting.

"What the fuck did you think you were doing in there?"

"Calm down," Ada said. "We're fine. It's okay."

"It's not okay! Why did you have to go and talk to that woman?"

"I was having trouble focusing at school, Asụghara, don't you remember? I just wanted to get it checked out."

"But that's not what she was talking about in there. She knew my name! What have you been telling her?"

"Nothing! Nothing much. She asked a few questions."

I shook my head. The damage was already done; all I could do was manage it from here. "Well, you don't need to go back," I told Ada.

She frowned. "The therapist said that sometimes it's going to feel like I don't need the help. She said I should ignore that feeling."

I rolled my eyes at her. "Don't be silly, you can't ignore me. I said you're not going back. Okay?"

"Look, I don't like it either, Asụghara, but I think it's a good idea to get some help."

"It's like you're not hearing me, Ada. I don't want you to see her again."

Ada set her jaw, getting ready to answer back, but I'd had enough of arguing with flesh. I collected power in my hand and ran it across the marble, sending a deep streak of pain through her skull. Ada gasped and clutched her head, but I didn't stop. I sank my fists into the marble and split her head open with a crashing migraine, and it worked. She never went back to that therapist again.

That was how I kept us all safe, from doctors and diagnoses and the medications they surely would've shoved into Ada if they ever saw exactly what her mind looked like. I needed her to rely on only me, so I could take her home and we could be with our brothersisters again and it would be as if none of this had ever happened. The way up is the way down.

It's not easy to persuade a human to end their life—they're very attached to it, even when it makes them miserable, and Ada was no different. But it's not the decision to cross back that's difficult; it's the crossing itself. I had high hopes, sha, since Ada was in a lot of pain. It was always easier to push my agenda when she was hurting, and to be fair, she was always hurting, but this one was different. This one was about Ewan.

Ada and Ewan had been on and off since her graduation, instant messaging and e-mailing each other, then finally meeting up on the coast of Texas, where he pressed her against a yellow soft-top Jeep and told her that he'd fallen in love with her from the moment he saw her, all the way back in that blue room. It was as if he'd forgotten that he left her in Virginia, back when he'd told her that it was his girlfriend who made him happy. Now he was full of fresh confessions.

"You're the woman I've dreamed about all my life, but I've got nothing to offer you," he said. He was drunk. "You deserve so much more than I can give. You make me feel like I can do anything I dream of."

The wind whipped dust around them. The town they were in was close to the southern border.

"I can't imagine my life if you're not in it."

Inside the marble, Ada turned and whispered to me. "He thinks I'm too good to be true," she said.

"You are," I answered sourly. I wasn't going to make the mistake of loving Ewan again. She could do it alone if she wanted. Me, I'd been on Skype with one of Ewan's friends just a few weeks before, watching the boy strip off his clothes, his eyes a narrow and hungry blue. We were in New Jersey because Ada was visiting some Christian friends of hers, sitting in the same room as these good girls while the boy stroked his erection in the Skype window. I kept the laptop screen angled away from them and I thought it was fucking hilarious—they would've lost their minds if they knew what I was looking at. Like most people, they kept thinking that Ada was still just Ada. I kept my headphones in as he shuddered and moaned, spilling semen over his tight stomach.

He and Ewan played tennis together in Texas, so I knew it could only go so far, but still, it was fun to play. I sent the boy pictures of Ada, her skin bared and brown.

"I haven't been working out as much as I used to," I added.

"You have the smoothest body I've ever seen," he said, and that was when I knew I could have him. It wasn't a surprise—it never is.

He was the one who picked Ada up from the airport in Texas and took her to Ewan. He even went out drinking with them that night and never mentioned to Ewan any of the obscene things he'd said and done over the flattened glass of a computer screen, all for me. I liked that boy. He was a bad person—he was almost as interesting as Soren. I would've liked to fuck him, but Ada had chosen Ewan and it was impossible to get away.

She was naïve, sha. She actually thought things would change after Ewan told her he loved her, but of course, they didn't. He still had his girlfriend and he acted as if his confession by the yellow Jeep never happened. I can say a lot about Ada, but even she has limits, so she ended things with him and Ewan didn't fight it. It was their second breakup if you count the one in Virginia, and honestly, I wouldn't have allowed all this nonsense back and forth if it had been anyone else. But it was Ewan, and so the wheel kept turning. This time there were no e-mails, there was no contact, and Ada found herself enveloped by her first real heartbreak. I tried to help, to distract her with new lovers, but she was inconsolable. The girl couldn't even listen to most of her music because he'd given it to her and all the songs reminded her of lying in bed with him when it was winter outside. It was pathetic. I had loved him too, in my way, but after he left, I knew it had been a mistake. Ewan was just a man, after all, just flesh—selfish and typical flesh upon that. Besides, he'd mostly been spending time with me, not her, and I didn't expect anyone to be able to see their filthy wants reflected in my eyes and still stay.

In the middle of Ada's pain, I kept looking for a window I could use to take her home. She didn't have the strength to fight me, and my plan could've worked then, except that one day, Ada got a phone call from a number she didn't recognize. When she picked up, Ewan's voice poured into her ear.

"My girlfriend and I broke up," he told her. "It had nothing to do with you. But you told me not to come back unless I was single and ready to fight for you, and I am."

I had no chance against that kind of declaration, and when I saw the amount of joy having Ewan back brought to Ada, I didn't even want to try. I'm cruel, yes, but I'm not that cruel. She was happy and he was different. I could tell because I didn't like this version of him. Back in Virginia, Ada never even had his phone number, but this time, Ewan was calling her every night. He couldn't sleep without hearing her voice, he told his mother about her, and when Ada was struggling with her classes, he stayed on the phone with her and told her how much he believed in her.

"He's rebounding," I told her. "Just wait."

"I know," Ada said, but she was in love with him. All I could do was watch.

Ewan told her about the holidays before he and the girlfriend split, when he would go back to Ireland and show all his friends Ada's pictures on Facebook. "I told them if I wasn't with my ex, I would marry this girl in a heartbeat."

Ada spoke to him every day and it was all fresh and new and pretty. It made her happy. One night, Ewan asked what the worst thing he ever did to her was, and Ada winced at the memory but she told him anyway, about the last time they slept together in Virginia.

"I told you I loved you," she said. "You told me to shut the fuck up."

I was surprised to hear her say that—I thought I had been the one who said it, not her. Maybe we were blurring more than I realized.

"It was really shitty," she was saying. "It made me feel . . ." She paused. Was there a word to describe that particular humiliation?

On the other end of the phone line, Ewan spoke into the silence. "I made you feel cheap," he said, and then he started crying. "That was all you ever asked me for—to never lie to you and never make you feel cheap. I'm so sorry, Ada."

I listened in amazement as he apologized for all the things he'd done to her. Ada listened with me, equally surprised.

"Maybe it's not such a bad idea to love him again," I said to her. "That's if you want."

Ada tilted her head and listened to him thoughtfully. "Actually," she said, "I'm not sure."

She kept considering, weighing this new Ewan, and along the way, he told her that he too had a private relationship with Yshwa. I rolled my eyes at this, but I knew it mattered to Ada, to be with someone who loved Yshwa like she did. That November,

Ada flew back to that little Texas border town to spend Thanksgiving with Ewan.

He was claiming that he'd loved her for a long time, but I knew Ewan. He would never have left the security of his old relationship if he hadn't known Ada's wild love would catch him. It was fine, it was human. No wahala. Besides, he did love her, perhaps with even more abandon than she loved him because, as he had predicted, she changed his life. There was no need to pretend with her because Ada already knew who he was at his worst, so instead Ewan tried to show her who he could be at his best. I kept waiting for his cruel hands, the version of him that I knew and loved, but all he gave Ada was gentleness.

The first time she climbed into bed with this new Ewan, Ada reached for me as usual, but for the first time since I had thundered through a window to rescue her, I wasn't there. I didn't come.

Ewan thrust inside her while Ada held back tears, panic screaming inside her stomach because it wasn't supposed to be like that, not with him, not with the one she loved who loved her. After he came, Ada started crying.

"What's wrong?" said Ewan, naked and frantic, holding her as she wept. "What happened?"

"They're not bad tears," she said, to calm him. "I've never had sex without a mask on before. There's always this other hard layer on top of the real me." Ada felt crazy trying to describe me and Ewan just held her tighter.

"You don't need a mask," he said. "I'm not going to hurt you anymore."

But she was wrong—they were bad tears, they were a panic attack that threw her back into the marble. Inside her head was the only real safety. Ewan was just a stranger to us. Vincent placed his hand on the center of Ada's back as the panic took over her chest.

"Breathe," he said.

I stood by, horrified, watching as she wept. She looked up at me, her eyes reddened.

"Where were you?" she gasped, splintering under Vincent's hand, pieces of her crawling on the floor. "Why did you leave me? You said you would never leave me! I was alone!"

I continued watching her and all I could think was that I was so afraid, and I had never been afraid before. "I couldn't find you," I whispered. "I didn't know where you were, Ada, I swear. I couldn't get to you."

She sobbed against the marble and my heart broke.

"Maybe because it was him?" I was guessing. "Maybe you didn't even know when you sent me away, but I swear, I didn't know how to find you." The guilt was too much. One simple promise—you will never have to feel them move in you. I will be there. I will be the one they push into because they cannot hurt me.

And now Ada had gone and fallen in love with a man who had the power to send me away. He was going to destroy her.

"He can't make us leave," said Vincent, because he could see through the back of my open brain. "We'll always be here with you, Ada. And if we sleep a little more because you have him, maybe that's a good thing. Even if he leaves, we'll be here to pick up your pieces. We'll always be here, yeah? We promise. Right, Asụghara?"

I nodded because my throat was too tight for words. This felt too much like the day I was born, the way she had been entered and hurt.

"You're safe now," I managed to say. "We're never going to leave you."

I knelt beside her and held her hand tightly in mine.

"Breathe," said Vincent.

It must've gotten better. I don't remember much—I was sleeping more, just like Vincent had predicted. I was giving Ada a life because Ewan made her happy, and honestly, the girl deserved a little happiness. He left Texas and moved outside Boston to be with her. They got their first apartment together there. He proposed in a library in Cambridge and they got engaged and Saachi was furious, but she thawed after she met him and realized that Ada was going to marry him whether Saachi approved or not. So Saachi flew herself and Añuli to Ireland to meet Ewan's family, who was throwing an engagement party for him and Ada. When they returned to the States, Ewan and Ada quietly got married in Manhattan, at City Hall, and Ewan had tears in his eyes when he said his vows. They moved to Brooklyn, enrolled in graduate school, got a cat and named it The Prophet Jagger.

I left Ada to her new family. When she came to sit with me in the marble, we talked like old friends, as if we'd never planned to kill each other.

"He wants us to be equal," she told me.

I crossed my legs and frowned. "Like how?"

Ada blushed. "Like during sex." I stared and she lifted her shoulders, then dropped them and hugged her knees. "You know, on plain footing. With no one having more power over the other."

I laughed. "But that's impossible."

Ada shrugged again and fiddled with a broken nail. "Who knows," she said.

"It doesn't work like that, Ada, not when the clothes come off."

"You mean, not when you're there."

Oh. I hadn't realized I was still helping her with that, but it made sense. I was automatic at that point, a shell she could drag over her, whether I was asleep or not. "I guess I'm always there when the clothes come off," I said. "The promise must be holding."

"Yeah," she said. "We can't change that?"

I shook my head and took her palm. "You're just not capable of it, sorry. Or rather, we're not capable of it." Ada watched my nails slide between her fingers as I massaged her hand. All my bones were slightly longer than hers.

"How are you?" she asked.

I gave her a look. "I'm fine. I come when you need me, like now."

Ada looked a little ashamed. "I'm sorry I haven't been around that much."

"It's fine," I said. "As long as you remember that we can't be separated, Ada. Without us, you're nothing—you won't feel anything, you won't see anything, you won't write anything. You have to be at peace with us, you hear? We're you."

"Yeah, I know I have to remember," she said. "Otherwise I wake up not knowing who I am."

"Exactly." I patted her hand. "We're the buffer between you and madness, we're not the madness."

She nodded. "Where's Saint Vincent?"

"He's sleeping. Do you want me to call him?"

"No, let him rest." She watched as I cracked her knuckles one by one. "I don't want to lose you," she said, her voice small.

"Biko, how many times do I have to tell you? We're not going anywhere." She made a face and I rolled my eyes. "Ada, stop feeling guilty about being happy with Ewan. We're fine."

She blushed and looked down. "He wants me to give myself to him completely."

I looked at her, confused. "What?"

"Completely. You know. All of me. Like how he's given himself to me."

I didn't like how she said it, with a tinge of hope, so I tried to be gentle. "Me, I don't think that's possible, sha."

"Why not? Isn't that what you're supposed to do when you're in love?"

I groaned and dropped her hand. "My friend, it has nothing to do with love."

She frowned. "What is it then?"

I looked at her, and I swear, if I could've freed Ada right then and there to love and be happy and normal, I would have. But I didn't start any of this and I didn't know how to stop it, only how to finish it.

"What is it?" she demanded.

I took a deep breath and hoped for grace. "Look, you can't give yourself to him because you're not yours to give. That's it. I'm sorry."

It took a minute for Ada to understand, to realize that she was locked away, that all those parts of her he wanted, the parts she wanted to give, the parts that would complete the love they had—all those parts were gone. Or if they weren't gone, they'd been put somewhere so far away that not even Ada could touch them, let alone Ewan. I watched her face fall, and when she started crying, I held her and whispered apologies for what felt like forever.

It was only a matter of time after that. Ewan wanted what any man in love would: a wife who could withstand tenderness, who didn't have the core of her locked away inside a dark ocean. He wanted a soft moon in his hands and he got a scalding sun. Ada didn't have a choice—she would have given him everything if she could, just to make him happy. He had stopped drinking for her, stopped smoking, stopped the drugs, everything. But I had made her a promise and we were both trapped inside it, doomed to play our roles without release. It broke her heart and I couldn't stand to see her in so much pain, so I took over and I took her away, because their marriage was burning and I was trying to protect her. It took Ada and I years to realize that I fucked it up, that keeping her walled off from Ewan killed any chance they had at making it out together. By the time Ewan was begging her, she was long gone and I refused him. But honestly speaking, even if she and Ewan had fought more, they probably still would've lost. The only thing that could've saved them was if I had never existed, if Ada was not divided up the way that she was, if she had been able to control me. We can stand here and list impossible things all day long.

By the time Ewan moved out of their apartment, he was drinking again, smoking packs of cigarettes, and snorting coke in small bathrooms in the West Village. He dropped out of school, leaving Saachi with a huge loan she'd cosigned for him, and then he fled the country. That was when I knew I had been right, that he had been weak the whole time, that it was a good thing Ada couldn't give herself to him, because he would have ruined her; he was nothing more than a fucking useless human.

It was time for me to come back and make it right. I had let Ada have her time in the sun. She had known love, she had tasted happiness, and it had gone bad. That was fine, that was life, abi? No wahala. But I still carried a larger truth, a better truth. It had been good to be flesh. It would be better to go home.

Chapter Fifteen

'Nwa anwụna, nwa anwụna': nwa nwụọ ka anyị mara chi agaghị efo.

Ada

My mother does not sleep at night.
She worries. This is the way of things
when cold gods give you a child.
I sleep like swollen opium.

She worries. This is the way of things.
I went mad so young, you see.
Sleeping like swollen opium,
screaming on my better days.

I went mad too young, you see,
they couldn't wait to ride me.
I only scream on my better days,
crippled in meat and hot skin.

They couldn't wait to ride me,
to drink from my terrible depths.
Crippled in meat and hot skin,
I tried to die from this body.

I drank from my terrible depths,
my mother cannot keep me safe.
I tried to fly from this body,
now clawed shadows follow her.

They slaver at the foot of her bed.
When cold gods give you their child,
make sure you keep her alive.
My mother does not sleep at night.

Chapter Sixteen

Your graveyard looks like a festival.

Asụghara

After Ewan left, I was tired, so I let Saint Vincent step to the front a little more. He dressed Ada in skinny jeans from Uniqlo, thick cotton T-shirts, and a binder—a tight black vest that flattened our chest into a soft mound of almost nothing. Saachi was frantic.

"You're in a dark place," she said over the phone. "You're unstable."

Ada laughed and ignored her. Saint Vincent went to clubs with satin-padded walls and red velvet curtains, where he kissed women with Ada's mouth. I calculated that if one tablet of the cyclobenzaprine prescribed for Ada's sciatica could knock her out for thirteen hours, then a whole bottle of them would easily take her home. Things started to tumble with an alarming speed. Ada checked herself into a psychiatric ward and I made her check out the next day. Chima flew into New York.

It was strange to see the bulk of him in Ada's small yellow kitchen. Ever since I was born, I hadn't paid much attention to Ada's flesh siblings; my brothersisters were far more interesting. But Chima and Añuli mattered very much to Ada and she was always involved in something with them, one small hot conflict or the other. She wanted Chima to save her, like a big brother, to protect her better than I was doing. She thought he was there because she'd been in the hospital, and in a way, he was.

"I have something to tell you," he said. "Mummy and I thought it was better if you heard it in person, since you just got out of the hospital."

Ada sat at her unstained Ikea kitchen table and looked across at her brother. I watched lazily, relaxed now that we weren't locked up in a fucking psych ward anymore. He was calm; Chima was always calm.

"Uche is dead," he said, and Ada's heart staggered.

Uche was Ada's cousin, the only son of De Simon, one of Saul's older brothers. When Ada was a child, before the rest of us woke up, she loved going to Umuahia, back to where she was born. One of her clearest memories there was of being summoned by the old men who sat under the tree by the road that turned into the family compound. They had examined her face closely, moving it to catch the light, veined hands directing her jaw.

"It's true," one of them said. "This one resembles nwa Simon."

The rest nodded in agreement and Ada felt warmth spread in her chest. Looking like Uche meant she belonged somewhere. It was like they were saying—we can see our blood in your face, you're one of ours. All the stories Ada knew about Uche had come from Chima in their childhood, what he overheard from Saul or Saachi, or pretended to know as the oldest child. That Uche lived in London. That Uche dated men. That Uche and De Simon had not spoken in over ten years. That Saachi didn't like how Uche and De Simon didn't speak.

When Ewan's family threw that engagement party in Dublin, Uche had flown in from London with his partner, a quiet Danish man called John, who worked with astronauts. I was dormant then, just watching Ada be happy. Once Saachi and Añuli arrived from the States, Añuli and John clicked right away. The two of them spent the engagement party blowing bubbles together in a corner. Uche was older now; his face was sharp with cheekbones and he had eagle eyes set under his eyebrows. Ada didn't look like her cousin anymore—the old men must have been thinking about when he was a child—but she and Uche danced together on the wooden spread of the dance floor, and later that year, he flew to the States and visited with Saachi and Añuli in the desert of the Southwest. After Ewan left, after everyone found out that Ada was dating women and flew into fits, Uche was the only one in the family who really understood, who loved her and said he was proud. He was meant to visit again, that November, he said, to New York, to see Ada, but he had a pulmonary embolism and fell down in London in October and died.

I was furious. It was as if staying alive just gave everyone else time to leave you. Chima stayed in New York for a few days and came to therapy with Ada.

"Do you know you haven't cried?" he said there. "You just keep smiling."

Ada smiled politely at him and the therapist. I kept my fingers hooked to the corners of her mouth until Chima left.

Later that year, Ada was at her girlfriend Donyen's apartment in Flatbush, speaking on the phone with Saachi. The Christmas presents Saachi had sent were spilling out of Ada's satchel, peanut M&M'S on the hardwood floor and a stocking full of fluffy mice and feathered sticks, toys that Saachi had sent for Ada's cats.

"I'm not wrapping up presents for pets," Ada was telling her mother, holding the phone to her ear with the lift of her shoulder. "It's ridiculous."

"Just hang up the stocking, lah," Saachi replied. Her voice crackled over the line. "Open it on Christmas Day."

Ada laughed and I smiled inside her. The whole conversation was silly, but sometimes even I felt reassured by how familiar Saachi's voice was, by how Ada could pick out her handwriting at a glance, how Ada's own handwriting was often mistaken for Saachi's, as if their connection showed in the ink.

"Were you the one who used the phone card?" Saachi asked, switching topics. All the children had the PIN for the card, for when they needed to make international calls, to Saachi's mother in Kuala Lumpur, to Saul back in Nigeria, wherever.

"It's not me," Ada said. "I think I used it last to call the UK." She crumpled some paper from the parcel. I yawned and stretched in her mind. "Wait," she continued, "actually, have you called Uche? You were supposed to. Did you call Uche?"

There was a pause on Saachi's end. "You mean John," she said.

I could feel Ada's shock in her throat. The last time she'd heard Uche's voice was when he was in the desert making fun of Añuli's fashion choices. She couldn't believe she'd forgotten that he was dead, instead of being out there somewhere with their shared blood under his face.

"Yes," she managed to choke out. "I meant John."

Ada dated Donyen until the end of the following summer. She still lived in the flat she'd shared with Ewan when they were married, exposed brick in the bedroom, high ceilings, a fuchsia accent wall. She had interesting new friends: people who could see past flesh; people who prayed to gods, were ridden by them; people who heard transmissions even if they didn't particularly want to listen in. Her friends began to tell her things.

"We're afraid for you," they said.

"It's like you're on this thin line between being alive and being dead, like one small shift could send you in either direction."

"The first time I met you, I told another friend that you were lovely, but that I had this feeling you would die soon."

I was impressed. It was nice to be seen. None of them could save Ada, sha. She was done for; she was mine. I would've killed her sooner, except that her grief over Ewan was a little addictive. She ran from it, and everywhere she ran was somewhere I loved, so I let her live. Donyen had loved her, but it was nothing like Ewan's love, and Ada had realized that the grief would find her whenever she was alone. So she drank a lot of tequila, pouring the golden burn of it down her throat till it held her from the inside out, tighter than anyone's arms ever could. She paid attention to the acid in a lime and the feel of rough green skin against her lips, the glow in her thighs when the alcohol took hold, the taste of blood orange and ice. In the bathrooms, she reeled and caught her palm on the walls as she squatted to pee, her vision unsteady, her smile shaken out as if her teeth were rattling seeds. I watched her laugh in the mirror as she washed her hands.

"You're sooooo drunk," she slurred, leaning into the mirror. I looked back out at her and laughed, delighted. We pushed the bathroom door open and disappeared into thumping beats on the dance floor. Another night, Ada sat at a bar where her friend worked, and this friend kept refilling our glass with the dregs of the drinks that had been mixed for other customers. Ada ended up riding the uptown train alone at two in the morning, and she was so gone that I had to force her to keep her eyes open—I knew we'd black out the moment she let them close. Still, being wasted felt wonderful, like I was drifting away from reality, floating in a separate and better space.

Back at her apartment, Ada broke open disposable razors to get to their flimsy blades. She cut her arm next to the old scars and watched the thin red lines form, the leaking full drops that suspended from her skin until she flicked them up with her tongue. She threw glasses against the wall and they shattered into thousands of fragments shining with angry points, a better future than being whole. It was all so much better than the grief.

When she sat in the marble with me, we looked more identical than we ever had, so close that Saint Vincent excluded himself from our conversation. Ada and I were drunk on homemade margaritas, using empty milk bottles as glasses.

"I've never understood," she said, "back when I was little, why Yshwa wouldn't come down to hold me, you know?"

"Oh, I know this one," I said, closing my eyes to feel the softness in my blood. "Because he's a useless asshole."

She ignored me. "Especially when he knew that I didn't have anyone else." Ada didn't sound sad, just matter-of-fact.

I relaxed all my limbs. "I know."

"But I'm older now," she continued.

"Correct."

"Okay, but listen, Asụghara." She leaned forward and I opened my eyes to look at her. "Now that I'm older, right, why won't he just kill me in my sleep?"

She pushed some hair out of her face and sat back. I wanted to tell her Yshwa was always going to disappoint her, but I took a sip of my drink instead. She could figure that out herself.

"It's basically the same thing," she said. "I didn't have anyone to hold me and now I don't have anyone to kill me. You'd think he'd come through on at least one of these points."

"That's not true," I said, and I leaned out to put my hand on her arm. "I'll kill you any day you want."

We stared at each other for a moment, then burst out laughing because we both knew I meant it. After our laughter died away, Ada and I leaned our backs against the marble and sighed together.

"Do you think about Soren a lot?" she asked.

I frowned. "Not really." I shifted my head to look at her. "You nko?"

Ada nodded. "I was thinking how this year makes it five years since you arrived," she said. "And then I was thinking of Ewan and I was remembering that night, in the fall, remember? When Ewan had come back and Soren was watching us."

"Ohhhh fuck, yeah. I remember. The house down the hill, that time when we were in Denis's room smoking."

"Yup. He used to ring that little bell when the joints were ready, remember? And then he'd play, like, Lauryn Hill or Hot Chip."

I laughed. "And Axel was there beating everyone at rock-paper-scissors. Everyone! It didn't make any fucking sense, he was so good at it."

Ada smiled, but she was thinking of Soren. "And then he came in and started talking to me, saying how I never used to smoke or drink, that he didn't want to think that I'd started now because of what he did. Can you imagine?"

"No, no, but you know what I loved?" I was giggling as I remembered. "Ewan tapped your shoulder and handed you the blunt, and you just looked at Soren like he was nothing, took it, and turned away from him. Finish."

"His face! He just walked out of the room." Ada was giggling now too. "Was that you or me?" she asked.

I shrugged and drank from my bottle. "Same difference."

"Oh my god, and remember the e-mail he sent a few months later?"

I made my voice high and whiny to mimic him. "'I never loved you. I was just missing my girlfriend.'"

Ada scoffed. "As if it mattered at that point."

"Eh, he was just trying to get to you."

Ada tilted her bottle up and pouted at me. "It's empty."

I reached over to touch the glass, and it filled back up with pink slush.

"What's that?"

"Strawberry this time," I said, and Ada laughed.

"This is why I keep you around."

I elbowed her and we drank in silence for a bit. "How come you're thinking about Soren?" I asked.

Ada sighed. "I'm pissed, I guess. It feels like he took something from me. I couldn't even be normal with Ewan. Like, what kind of wife can't make love to her own husband?"

I flinched. "Can we just say 'fuck'? You know how I feel about calling it that."

"You know what I mean. Have emotional sex."

"We did have emotional sex," I countered. "There were a lot of emotions involved in our fucking, thank you very much."

"Not that kind of emotion. I meant like tenderness."

I flinched again. "Seriously, Ada, or I'll take your drink away."

She laughed. "Okay, okay. You're fucking weird." A pause, and then she changed the subject. "Sometimes when I think about you, I can see you standing right next to me and it's like we're twins."

I gave her a look. "You know we're identical, right?"

She shushed me with her hand. "Except, when you're standing next to me, you're all covered in blood."

I drank some more. "That seems accurate."

"You'd be like the older twin, though, because you take care of me."

"I'm not very good at that."

Ada shrugged. "Eh. In your own way."

I changed my drink to straight tequila. "No, I'm good at hurting people and leaving people, and I'm really good at hiding you so that nobody can get you again."

"And you're good at fucking," Ada added, holding her bottle out to me.

I clinked mine to hers in salute. "And I'm good at fucking."

"And making them feel special."

"Oh, I'm reaaallly good at that." I smiled at her, but it was bitter and she knew it.

"You did your best, Asụghara."

"Yeah." I looked into my bottle. "I shouldn't even have existed."

"Oh god, are you getting to the sad drunk stage?" Ada reached for my bottle and I hugged it to my chest.

"Fuck off!"

She laughed. "Okay, stop whining then. You had to exist. I wasn't ready."

"But, like, you should've been, you know? You should've had time to do it when you were ready, not the way it happened." I was getting a little sad. Maybe her grief was contagious. I was remembering the day she realized it wasn't her fault, three years after I arrived, when she read the definition of rape online and burst into tears in Ewan's garden in Dublin, crying and crying as he held her.

"You should've had a chance to be ready," I said.

Ada sipped her drink, tilting her head back. "Shit happens," she said.

"Okay, now you sound like me."

"Hah. I'm just trying to be at peace. If I don't, I'll end up blaming Soren for me losing Ewan and that kind of makes me want to find the bastard and stab him in the face."

I tapped my bottle against hers. "Shit, I'm down with that."

Ada smiled and put her head on my shoulder. "Don't leave me," she said. "I don't think anyone else will want me without you."

"Don't say that."

"It's true. I'm the damaged and broken one; you're the bright and shiny one. Who are they going to love more? They don't have to do any work with you."

"I'm not going to leave you, but then you have to come with me, okay?"

"Come where?"

I exhaled. "You know where."

Ada hesitated. "It's just that I'm scared, Asụghara. I want to, but what if it doesn't work?"

I put down my bottle and put my arm around her. "I know," I said, and we sat together for a long time, saying nothing.

Ada surrendered to me in October, a year after Uche died. She was seeing a man named Hassan then, a capoeira teacher who she'd met at a club in Harlem during her breakup with Donyen. It was on a night when I was out hunting in her body, and Hassan had been standing by the club exit, dressed in tight black, his hair pouring down his back. I let him take Ada to his apartment, where he danced in his living room, his locs flying in the air. He kept talking the whole time, hard and fast, and his words jumped and scattered and cartwheeled. I was tired of them, so I climbed into the stretch of his black satin bed and watched him pull off his shirt. He was still talking.

"Shut up and fuck me," I said.

I remember how he stopped, shocked, before he gathered himself and climbed onto the bed with me. For the rest of the night I got to be myself in my meaty form, doing meaty things. I didn't have to think about Ada losing Ewan and neither did she, so it was good. It was a white blank space of pleasure and I felt free inside it.

The morning that Ada's surrender happened, she was sad because she'd had a fight with Hassan the night before. I was tired of everything, tired of the number of times I was going to have to watch her be in pain. So I sat her down in her yellow kitchen and splayed her out on a chair. She propped up her elbows on the raw wood of the kitchen table, stained with old splatters of turmeric and tomato. Uche's corpse sat across from her, his lung clot turning him gray as he watched her with gutted eyelids and still blood. Ada stirred miso paste and dehydrated seaweed into a bowl of hot water, talking softly to him as if he was alive. I stood behind her with my palm on her shoulder.

"Where did they put you?" she asked. "Tell me and I'll come find you."

I purred in her wrists. I was keeping a fine balance by bringing Uche's shade here, maintaining a delicate tension between Ada's world and that of the brothersisters.

"I'm sorry I didn't come sooner," Ada said. "They stopped me. And I know you'll want me to stay with them, but Uche, honestly, I don't want to anymore." She stopped stirring for a moment. "I wish I could tell them that."

I watched as Ada reached for her prescription bottle, pressed down and turned, popping the lid open. They were painkillers—Donyen had taken away all the muscle relaxants after she heard about the suicide plan. I tried refilling the prescription, but Ada gave it to Hassan because he had a thing for pills and injections, so all we had left were the painkillers. I figured we could manage with them.

"I wish I could've said good-bye to everyone without them freaking out, you know? No crying, no trying to lock me up. As if I was just traveling. Plus, there's no need for them to worry—I've got family waiting."

Uche's corpse leaned back and extended a long leg toward her refrigerator, folding its arms. A large flake of skin hung precariously off the steep height of its cheek.

"Alexander Uncle, Bishop Uncle, Grandpa, you." Ada looked up at Uche's corpse as she listed Saachi's dead family and frowned. "I feel you'll either be the most welcoming or the most angry." Her face crumpled into sadness at even the thought of it. "Don't be angry at me, please," she said. "I've had too much of it down here. I know I'm too much and everyone is tired of it, especially me. And I know the others care, but they'll stop me and I just want to lose, just this once."

She spilled the pills on the table, above the bowl and next to the open packet of freeze-dried strawberries. Uche's corpse dropped its heavy-lidded eyes to the pool she'd just made. I followed its gaze, looking down at the thousands of milligrams that were on our side. We couldn't lose, not this time.

I leaned into Ada's ear. "You know how they say take things a day at a time?" I said. "You can manage a pill at a time."

Ada nodded and I kept the count for her. A few hundred milligrams down, several thousand, a few hundred more to go. She always hated taking tablets with water and she'd meant to make grapefruit juice earlier, but the juicer was dirty. The dishwashing liquid was grapefruit scented. She tipped the bowl of miso soup to her mouth. When she was a child, Ada used to take medicine with chocolate milk, or else it would all come pouring thickly back up. I kept count for her.

A few thousand and a few hundred down. The trick, I had realized, was to get Ada to pretend that none of this was happening. Because if it was happening, she'd have to call her best friend, and what could that one do except worry from far away? So I made the kitchen unreal and Uche was there to prove it. If you die in a video game, do you die in real life? She had practice in the unreal from all those years of fairies, all those years of believing in floating lands and split selves; they were preparing all for this moment, this true attempt, this ultimate belief. I kept the count for her.

More thousands, more hundreds of milligrams. We were halfway done. Ada thought of Bassey Ikpi and her fifteen-year-old friend who killed herself. There was a whole nonprofit now named after her, the Siwe Project. She thought of all the gay kids who had killed themselves back to back that year, including the young man she spoke to on the train in Brooklyn, who'd gone home and hanged himself. The unseen and hurting ones, all leaving together. It felt like she had missed a train and was trying to catch up, slipping on the tracks.

I kept the count going. We had spent entirely too long with a foot in this world; the hold had to give, the foot had to return. The Obi may kneel down, but it never crumbles.

Hassan spoiled everything by calling her.

I watched it fall apart from there. I watched Ada talk to Hassan as if nothing had happened, as if Uche hadn't been and then not been in her kitchen, as if the unreal I'd spent all morning building hadn't just been destroyed. Right before she got off the phone, she told him.

"I think I did something stupid," she said, only calling it that because she knew that's what he would call it.

"What did you do?"

". . . I took some pills."

"What?"

"I took some pills."

"Some? How many did you take?"

Ada said nothing.

"How many did you take, Ada?!"

She tried to make it sound like a joke. "Um, quite a lot."

"What the fuck?!"

"No, no, it's fine. Let me call you back. I'm going to call one of my friends and sort it out." Ada hung up on him and turned on her computer. I watched, frozen. Just like that. Everything, gone. She was video chatting now, explaining what happened to one of her friends, being bright and chirpy in a way that was probably obscene.

Her friend was panicking. "Should I call 911?" she kept asking.

"No!" At least Ada and I were still on the same page with that. "Don't call anyone. It's going to be fine. I'm just going to make myself throw up—I didn't take that many. It'll be fine. Hold on."

I followed Ada numbly to the bathroom and watched her stick her fingers down her throat. Nothing came up but a piece of seaweed and some bile. She kept trying for about ten minutes, then went back to the computer and kept talking to her friend.

"I was just having a bad morning, like I was tired of everything—" Ada was interrupted by a banging on the front door and her friend started crying.

"I'm sorry," she said to Ada. "I had to call them."

Ada burst into short and panicked sobs. "No, no, no!" She slammed the laptop shut and I stepped in quickly, smoothing out her face so we could answer the door.

"Don't let them see you like this," I told her. I could barely feel anything—my failure was overwhelming—but we were still alive, and I still knew my job. Three police officers came in and started asking questions as I watched.

"Why would you go and do something like that?" one of them asked, amused. "Things can't be that bad."

I put a smile on Ada's face and she kept it as she looked at him, as she walked down the stairs and out to the sidewalk, where the ambulance was waiting for her. Donyen jumped out of a taxi and came up to Ada.

"Your friend called me," she said. "Told me you didn't want her to call 911 and I told her to call them. I told her, 'Do you want Ada to be mad at you or do you want her to be dead?' I'm coming with you."

I kept a smile stuck on Ada's face as they both climbed into the back of the ambulance. I had failed. Already, I knew that a second chance would be much harder to come by. But for now I had to handle the crisis I'd thrown us into. I did it with that same smile, joking with the nurses till they got irritated. One of them was Nigerian, and she scolded Ada without sympathy, forcing her to drink liquid charcoal. I watched Ada vomit it up into a white toilet bowl. I watched as she became delirious, as she panicked, as her other friends came and sat on her hospital bed. They sent a psychiatrist to come and evaluate her, but he didn't like our attitude and I could tell that he wanted to lock us up. That sobered me up faster than anything else would have. There was no way I was ever letting someone commit us, not after that night in the ward the year before.

"Let me handle it," I told Ada, even though we were both exhausted.

Donyen had gotten Hassan's number from someone else and called him behind Ada's back, yelling at him for not being there. I was furious when Hassan told us.

"You had no right to call him," I told Donyen, Ada's hospital gown crinkling at our shoulders. "It's none of your business."

"Are you serious?" she said. "You were calling his name, did you know? When you were delirious. You were calling his name and he can't even fucking come and see you?"

I took a deep breath. It was so fucking inconvenient to be dealing with this right when the doctors were trying to decide whether to discharge Ada or dump her in a psych ward. I wanted to slap Donyen. "You're my ex!" I snapped. "You can't be calling the person I'm seeing now to shout at him. And now I have to handle this shit in the middle of everything else because you can't mind your fucking business."

Hassan had been upset on the phone when he finally got through to Ada. "I can't do this shit," he said. "Your ex is fucking crazy."

"Dude," I told him, "you don't have to come to the hospital." The last time he'd been in one was when his mother had died. He'd been avoiding them since.

He showed up anyway, to tell Ada that he wanted to break up. I almost laughed. She was in a hospital bed after my suicide attempt and now she was getting dumped. Wonderful.

"Can you meet the doctor with me?" I asked him. "You were the last person I was with before it happened. I need someone to vouch for me."

So Hassan sat next to Ada across from the doctor, and he and I both turned on the charm, smiling and downplaying everything.

"I've had eight friends come in over the past twelve hours," I told the doctor. "Do you really think it's in my best interests to be separated from my support system and admitted into a ward without any form of outside communication instead of being released into their custody?"

She tapped on her desk. "The doctor who evaluated you felt you might be a risk to yourself," she said.

I smiled, and it was broad and confident. "I was a little groggy when he was asking me questions and he seemed a bit irritated, I don't know why. But you can see for yourself that I'm in good hands."

Hassan stepped in with his bright teeth and assured her that yes, Ada was in good hands, she'd been fine when he saw her the night before, and it was all just a rough morning. "She'll be okay, we'll take care of her," he lied.

Donyen had already walked out in a temper before he arrived. "I know I abandoned you," she said later. "I was angry. I'm sorry."

The doctor discharged Ada, to my collapsing relief. Sạachi had been calling but I wouldn't take her calls or Chima's. She called one of Ada's friends instead. "She needs to stay in the hospital," Saachi said. "Let me talk to her doctors."

She couldn't. I'd had Ada revoke all Saachi's access back when she started calling us unstable, so she wasn't Ada's emergency contact anymore, and since this was America, the doctors refused to talk to her. "We don't have the patient's permission," they said. Later in the evening, Ada spoke to Añuli.

"Are you okay now?" Añuli asked.

"Yeah, I'm good," Ada lied.

"Okay. Good."

That was it. Just like that, I had lost.

Chapter Seventeen

How many days are we going to use
to count the teeth of the devil?

We

Tell a child to wash her body and she washes her stomach. Asụghara was a fool for what she tried. Of all the paths she could have chosen, she went and picked the one that was taboo to Ala, as if she would be allowed to complete it, as if she forgot whose child the Ada was. Life does not belong to us to take. And on top of that, she should have remembered that we are ọgbanje; none of us die like this.

It had been a good gamble nonetheless, having the little beastself out in the world, allowing her to leap from bed to bed and shake hearts between her pointed teeth. When she failed at returning through the gates, we felt the sting of it strongly. If Ala did not want us to return yet, then we had been disobedient by trying. The brothersisters were no excuse, even though they had commanded us to come back—between them and her, the choice of who to obey shouldn't have been a choice.

So we were still caged inside the Ada, with the grainy memory of charcoal coating the back of her throat. She was more isolated than ever and we were chafing at still being flesh, so the only thing left to do was hunt. If we were trapped in a body, then we would do bodily things. We painted the Ada's mouth and lined her eyes with night, and we went out with Asụghara on a long and relaxed leash. It was easy, as it always was. At the bar, there was a man with eyes like anchors and hair like snakes, and although he was shy there, he held the Ada's hand when she got out of the taxi and walked with him to the brownstone he lived in. What a gentle strange thing, we thought. We felt large and cruel next to him, Asụghara hiding behind the sweet of the Ada's face, puzzled by his delicacy. In his apartment, we watched as he moved around his shelves and furniture. He was a craftsman and there were fine things everywhere. The Ada said something that amused him and he took her face in his hands, laughing, and kissed her in a pure and glimmering moment.

In the tightness of his bedroom, Asụghara put our palm against the red houndstooth wall and cried out as he moved in the Ada. The flesh was flesh, and for a little while, we could forget all the hurt, all the weight of over two decades of embodiment destroying us. He was so beautiful.

"You don't have to be gentle," Asụghara told him. He looked in our eyes, raised his hand, and hit us hard across the Ada's face. The impact rattled her jaw, but we didn't look away;

we felt the taste of rain fill our mouth. Ah, he was such a gentle, strange thing, to hurt us so perfectly. In the morning, before his reality descended on him again, he turned his head to the Ada.

"I needed this," he whispered. "I needed you."

She had forgotten his name, if she ever knew it, and we never heard from him again. Months later, when the summer was starting and Brooklyn was spilling sunshine, the Ada ran into him at a street festival and he lowered his anchor eyes as he passed. We forgave him easily. After you have let the wilderness in you come out and play, after you have spilled your darkness in front of a stranger, it can be difficult to look at them in the sentience of daylight. Besides, he was only a beautiful blip in the crazed timeline of embodiment—he mattered so much, and yet, not at all.

In the months since we'd been in his bed, the Ada had been to Lagos, to Cape Town and Johannesburg, where Asụghara had taken bodies in backseats and hostel beds and living room floors. We had overreacted and scared the humans, forgotten their names and faces, betrayed some friends and left others. Even all of that was nothing compared to the best thing we'd accomplished, when we laid out the Ada's body on a surgical table and let a masked man take a knife lavishly to the flesh of her chest, mutilating her better and deeper than we ever could, all the way to righteousness. After such carvings, how could one human matter?

* * *

The Ada's surgery happened the spring after Asụghara's failed attempt, just five months later. Before then, we used to think of the body as belonging truly to the Ada, as something that we were only guests in, something that the beastself could borrow. But now that we had been spurned from the gates, now that we were sentenced to meat, it was time to accept that this body was ours too. And with Saint Vincent, our little grace, taking the front more than he used to, the body, as it was, was becoming unsatisfactory, too feminine, too reproductive. That form had worked for Asụghara—those breasts with the large, dark areolae and nipples she could lift to her mouth—but we were more than her and we were more than the saint. We were a fine balance, bigger than whatever the namings had made, and we wanted to reflect that, to change the Ada into us. Removing her breasts was only the first step.

You must understand, fertility was a pure and clear abomination to us. It would be unthinkable, unbelievably cruel for us to ever swell so unnaturally, to lactate, to mutate our vessel. Could there be anything more human? The ways of our brothersisters, of ọgbanje, were clear. Do not leave a human lineage, for you did not come from a human lineage. If you have no ancestors, you cannot become an ancestor. We were happy to obey these instructions; we had always ferociously protected the Ada from the blasphemy of having another life grow in her. How many times had Asụghara allowed a wash of sperm into the Ada's body? Yet each time, we hardened against it and nothing took. We were a miracle like that, a mercy to the Ada.

When Ewan left and Asụghara allowed Saint Vincent to take the Ada's body and start binding her chest—all of these things were in preparation for a shedding, the skin splitting in long seams. The first time the Ada wore the binder, she turned sideways in a mirror and Saint Vincent laughed out loud in relief, in joy, in the rightness of the absence. The Ada was wearing faded purple jeans, and the soft of her belly swelled out from under the cutting bottom edge of the vest. But she could endure that, even the sharpness around her armpits. The flatness was worth it. The Ada pulled a short-sleeved T-shirt over the vest and ran her hands up and down the mild curve. It felt like armor, like we were bulletproof, like Saint Vincent was being built up in layers of determined fiber. The Ada wore the binder every day and washed it by hand in her small bathroom sink. Once, she made the mistake of putting it in the dryer, weakening the elastic. Saint Vincent suffered with each fraction of looseness she had caused, so she was more careful after that.

Before Asụghara put us in the emergency room, we had been searching for doctors to alter the Ada, to carve our body into something that we could truly call a home. Saachi finally realized, in her panic over the Ada's suicide attempt, exactly how much of her daughter actually belonged to her, which was to say, not much at all. The Ada was slipping from the human mother to us, to a freedom Saachi didn't trust. After all, how could she keep the girl safe if the girl wouldn't listen, wouldn't obey, if the girl was us? We were grateful that Saachi had at one time cared for the Ada, had kept her alive as a baby and been an excellent guardian as far as she could, but what did she know of graces or beastselves or ugly, unwelcome embodiments or the sacrifices a snake must go through to continue its timeline, the necessity of molting, the graves built of skins? We ignored her as gently as we could—this body was ours, not hers; this girl was ours, not hers, she had to understand where her jurisdiction ended and how pushing further was blasphemy.

The Ada used a therapist to assist with our carving plan and we discovered that humans had medical words—terms for what we were trying to do—that there were procedures, gender reassignment, transitioning. We knew what we were planning was right. Even the things that the Ada used to dislike about her body had mellowed out once we let Saint Vincent run. Then, the broad shoulders and the way they tapered down to narrow hips and small buttocks finally fit. Men's clothes draped properly on this body—we were handsome. We considered removing the breasts utterly and tattooing the flat of her chestbone, but that decisiveness still felt wrong, one end of the spectrum rocketing unsteadily to the other end—it wasn't us, not yet. So we chose a reduction instead of a removal; we cut down the C cups of blatant mammary tissue to small As, flat enough to not need brassieres, to not move, to be a stillness. The Ada wanted to include her human mother in the carving and we allowed it because, we supposed, vessels are loyal. But Saachi was against the surgery—she called the doctors and threatened them till they pulled out; she fought with the therapists, fought to have us seen as unstable, sick. She called Saul, who she never spoke to, not since the divorce, and told him, outed us to him.

"Your daughter is trying to cut off her breasts," she said.

The Ada was furious but we remained calm. We understood what was necessary—humans often fail at listening, as if their stubbornness will convince the truth to change, as if they have that kind of power. They do, however, understand forceful things, cruelties—they obey those. So we terminated Saachi's contact with the Ada's doctors, we excluded her, exiled and excommunicated her. This was when she stopped being an emergency contact; this was why she had no access to the Ada's doctors when Asụghara tried to kill the body. For a woman who looked to drown her loneliness in her children, it was a brutal thing to do, to push her out. But we had to strip her of power, to remind her that a mere human could not thwart us, that she stood no chance. Wẹ do not return your children until it suits us, if ever.

When we found the next doctors, the human mother knew nothing about it. The Ada brought in pictures of small chests, small enough to where we didn't think of them as breasts, small enough to where we could feel reverted to a time when we weren't capable of biological things, when we were neutral like we should have been. The Ada hoarded her student loan refunds until she had enough: thousands to pay the doctor and the anesthesiologist. She braided long yarn onto her locs so they could be tied back and left alone as we recovered from the surgery.

Saachi called the Ada, unaware of the plan, excited for a visit she was planning to see her sister. "I'm coming to New York," she said. "I need to get a visa for China."

The Ada began to panic but we brushed her aside. It was an unnecessary reaction—what a waste of time to spend it being human. We wrote to Saachi and informed her that the Ada was getting an operation the day before Saachi's flight would arrive.

"You are welcome to stay at the apartment if you're going to be supportive," we wrote. "Otherwise, you have to stay at a hotel." It was simpler this way. We were an inevitable force; it would be easier to fall into our flow than to question things. Like we said, she needed to understand. The girl belonged to us, had always belonged to us.

On the day of the surgery, the doctor drew thick black lines over the Ada's chest. He explained how he was going to make incisions in the underneath fold of the breast, slice up the middle, ring the nipple in a smooth, round, and bloody cut. The fatty tissue would be removed; the dark circle of areolae would be made small, tiny, a bare orbit around the nipple. The gashes would be stitched with a material that the flesh would take in later so it wouldn't have to be taken out. Pictures were taken. They slid a thin and strong length of hollow metal into the Ada's arm and fed her drugs through it. She had never been sedated before; we had known nothing of the taste of such drugs since the days we were born, and it was a strange artificiality as we counted down, as we went absolutely nowhere. There were no gates, no middle spaces—we were just gone and then we were back and it was hours later and we were missing weight from our chest.

Saachi arrived the next day and said nothing about the surgery, asked no questions. We approved of her decision. She accompanied the Ada to the post-op appointment, to the clean, organized waiting room, then back to the exposed brick of the Ada's apartment and her yellow kitchen. She helped the Ada change the dressings and caught her arm when the heat from the shower made our body faint. It was a relief; we were grateful for the reprieve, not for us, no, but for the Ada. Malena was there as well, witness as she always was, and the Ada smiled to see her mother share Heinekens and Dominican cigars with this her saintridden friend. As for us, we were fascinated by the white tape that hid the cuts, by the fine stitching, by the new body. We juggled the Ada's chemistry and decided to purify her: we ran through her cells and rejected alcohol, meat, dairy, processed sugars; we made them cramp her stomach, hurt her head, and twist her intestines. This was our body and it would become what we wanted, now that the reconfiguring was done.

Before the surgery, the Ada had told her friends that she couldn't wait for when she could wear dresses again. They were confused. They stared at her bound chest and boy clothes.

"Why would you go more feminine without boobs?" they asked. "Most people get it done to be more masculine."

The Ada shrugged and we moved in her shoulders. It was simple how we saw ourself, dresses creeping up the thigh, gashing open at the front to show chest bone—tulle and lace and clouds of clothes. Just like how having long hair weighing down our back made us want to wear buttons up to our throat, men's sleeves rolled up our biceps, handsome, handsome things. None of this was a new thing. We had been the same since the first birth, through the second naming, the third molting. To make the vessel look a little more like us—that was the extent of our intent. We have understood what we are, the places we are suspended in, between the inaccurate concepts of male and female, between the us and the brothersisters slavering on the other side.

After our first birth, it took only a short time before we realized that time had trapped us in a space where we no longer were what we used to be, but had not yet become what we were going to be. It was a place that always and never moved. The space between the spirits and the alive is death. The space between life and death is resurrection. It has a smell like a broken mango leaf, sharp, sticking to the inner rind of our skin.

The prophecies that came later, from Malena and others, they explained this—the shifting, the quick skinnings and reshapings, the falling and revival of the scales. But by then it was too late for the Ada to do anything except try to keep up with us, try not to be drowned in the liminal fluid we swam in. It tasted sharp as gin, metallic as blood, was soaked in both, down past the red into the deep loam. Ọgbanje space. We could rest in it like the inside curve of a calabash; we could turn in on ourself, wind back to our beginning, make those final folds. Sometimes they call this the crossroads, the message point, the hinge. It is also called flux space, the line or the edge—like we said, resurrection.

Chapter Eighteen

My god, my god.

We

There had been, in all of this, some comfort in knowing that we were not the first to pass through and wake up in flesh. Since the baptism, since they called him up from the acid of the sea with prayer, we'd known about Yshwa. He remained throughout the years, drifting by and over, his face shifting, the bones underneath bubbling and moving. We understood Asụghara's resentment of him, for his refusal to take flesh again for the Ada, but his choice made sense. It has always been obvious that Yshwa, like other gods, is not moved by suffering in the ways humans imagine.

Perhaps he would take flesh one last time, when the world was ending, just to watch it burn. Or he might continue to stay away, despite how many people awaited his glorious redescent. If we were him, we would do that, stay away. Why exist in this realm by choice? Humanity was ugly and cratered; it made sleep a relief, a brief escape where we could slide into another realm. That was as close to death as we could get, as close to the gates, to returning home or anywhere else. If we had been released like Yshwa, no amount of praying or fasting or midnight vigils would bring us back, no matter how much olive oil or blood was spilled in our name. But that was not what happened.

We remained trapped and so Asụghara softened toward Yshwa as he kept visiting the marble for his meetings with the Ada. At first, Asụghara would turn away and pretend not to hear the soft ripple of their conversations, the only form of prayer the Ada was capable of anymore. Ever since Soren, she couldn't kneel or press her palms together to worship Yshwa the way she used to—it felt false. Too much had been broken. So the Ada simply spoke to him as they took walks along grassed paths and black beaches, where they would sit on sea bones and watch the water.

Yshwa was different every time he manifested. He used variations of his original human form, changing the height, the degree of brown in his skin from mild to deep, the cleanliness of his linens, the kink of his dark hair, the breadth of his nose. His hands would be long fingered with smooth, pearled nails, or broad and stocky with callused palms that he picked splinters out of as they spoke. Sometimes he was tall, thin, with a graceful neck and tired eyes, his skin black as stone. Or he'd be thick, barrel-chested, thighs like foundations, skin like burnt sugar. He was always gentle.

When Asụghara started to turn toward him, slowly and hesitantly, Yshwa called no attention to it. He continued the conversations as if he'd been speaking to both Asụghara and the Ada all along, as if he'd always known the beastself was listening and his words had been meant for everyone. We approved of Asụghara's change of heart because, after all, Yshwa understood better than anyone what we were going through, having died in his own flesh form, and having him was better than being alone here. Besides, since his embodied days had been so long before ours, we could accept him as an older sibling. It was nice to have another brothersister.

We tried to teach ourself to see humans as he did, with the same grace, to follow his example. After Soren and the loss of her faith, the Ada had decided that her life was better with Yshwa in it after all. It didn't matter to her if he was real; she believed that the church around him was irrelevant, and she hoped that her afterlife would be one of oblivion. The Ada chose him because she needed a moral code to control us with, one that could protect her and others from our hungers. Yshwa had a good code, a simple one: love. Still, we found it difficult, unnatural even, to embrace his ways. The only vessel we truly cared about was ours: the Ada. Apart from her, we did hold Saachi in some regard for being the container of a universe, and Añuli for being Añuli. The Ada, however, cared about more than those two—she cared about Saul and Chima, about her friends; she had a long list of loved ones. We did not, as the beastself had demonstrated with Itohan's older brother in Georgia, and were not inclined to—most of what we knew of humans was what the beastself knew, that they were cruel, that their world was cruel, that everyone was, inevitably, going to turn into dust. We could see the logic of the beastself's philosophy—to hunt and feed on bodies, to use them in wringing out pleasure, to put that before anything, because otherwise, why were we alive and what was the point?

But it was not the using of humans that alarmed the Ada enough to try and guide us with a code. It was the places we went for pleasure with Asụghara guiding us—the ecstasy we felt in tricking humans and watching their heartbreak, watching them crumple against walls, seeing the shocked pain in their eyes. We had no remorse; we left that to the Ada. We became complicit in many betrayals, met men who lied and devastated their women, who despised humans like we did, who acted like they were gods and not humans. We let Asụghara play with these men, and when she was tired of batting them around and baiting them with the Ada's heart, we helped her remind them that divinity was deliberately not accorded to all flesh, that they were nothing, no better than the women they thought they could injure. The men all confessed their love to the beastself, with their mouths or with hunger in their eyes after she left them, after she threw them all away. The Ada suffered in this because, like a human, she had loved some of them.

When we were faced with Yshwa, it was easy to justify the things we had done. We did not care. The Ada wanted to be contrite. Asụghara wanted to burn the world down. We were guilty only of allowing the beastself to run the body into mattresses and hearts. What did it matter?

"You are weak with lust," Yshwa told us.

"Argue with the beastself," we said, and we left Asụghara out for him.

She shrugged. "They are only humans."

"You're no better," he countered. "Driven by instinct, incapable of restraint, ruled by desire."

Asụghara hissed, offended. "You don't understand—" she began, but Yshwa raised a hand to silence her.

"You forget," he said. "I once had a body too."

The silence that fell was weighted. "I just want to be free," Asụghara said eventually.

We wondered if she meant from us, if she wanted to be a separate self, with her own body, doing as she pleased. If so, she would have to learn, as the Ada had, what things in this life were impossible. The whole is greater than the individual.

"I thought you wanted to follow my teachings," Yshwa said, but he meant all of us, not her.

We hesitated. The Ada wanted to follow him, that much was clear; she had never tried to steer all of us as firmly as she was attempting now, but we were many and she was small.

"Don't ask me to stop for the humans," Asụghara spat. "Taking from them is the only pleasure we have left."

"You can't lean on that forever," Yshwa said.

"Do you have a better plan? Do you know how to make the pain stop?"

It was only with eyes like ours that we saw Yshwa flinch, just with fractions of his skin, as if he was remembering. "It doesn't."

Asụghara spoke for us. "Then we won't either."

He came up and laid his hand on her cheek. It burned, and she turned into the Ada. "Do it for me," he whispered.

The Ada's eyes filled with tears. "It's not fair, Yshwa. We just want it to stop hurting. Or have you forgotten? At least you got to die."

She wanted to look away—we wanted to look away—but Yshwa held her face tight. His breath felt like a thousand tiny cuts against our skin.

"We're gods," he reminded her. "I don't have to be fair." When he pressed his mouth to her forehead, our bones boiled underneath. The Ada closed her eyes. "I will lead you," he whispered, "down the paths of righteousness for nothing, other than the sake of my name." When we looked up again, he was gone.

It was not the last time he tried to save us, to pull us out of our own condemnation and wrap us in his peace. Yshwa knew the Ada's secret fear—that she had become evil because of the things Asụghara had done.

It didn't matter. He was not enough.

We stopped hunting because it had lost its shine, but we could not give Yshwa what he wanted. There was too much safety in sin, too much sweetness to walk away from. We took lovers who belonged to other people, kissed husbands after the sun had set and also in the broad brightness of afternoon. We gave the Ada new men, not entirely reformed, but not as cruel as the ones before them. She felt a little safer with these ones, so she wrote about them to Yshwa, like evidence of small remedies, proof that she was slowly, somehow, being saved.

Chapter Nineteen

You cannot find it. And if you find it, you cannot touch it.

Ada

Dear Yshwa,

I am lying in bed in my lover's shirt. He always leaves something behind, but he doesn't mean to. The first time it was that navy cardigan, the one I wore till he came back. The sleeves were too big and they swallowed up my elbows.

Yesterday, when he left, I walked him to the train and he kissed me on the platform. I watched the train pull away and then I walked back up the stairs, across the concrete of the plaza. I walked through the battered white door of my building and up the rickety stairs to my apartment. His white T-shirt was lying on my bed. It smelled like him. I stripped off my clothes and pulled it over my body. I slept in his scent.

I love him, but not too much. Carefully. He doesn't touch me when he sleeps but he holds me against him when he's awake.

It is simple with him. There's fun, good friendship, and powerful orgasms. Sometimes, it feels like I don't need anything else.

"I don't believe in missing people," he tells me. "If I miss you, I can just call you."

He's rarely in the country when he calls. I love him, but just enough.

"Look at this," he says, watching us in the mirror, our skins wet and gleaming. "This is so fucking beautiful."

Don't get me wrong. I still want forever, Yshwa. But I've learned that you can't force forever on the wrong people. They belong exactly where they are, giving exactly what they want to. I don't ask for anything more. I figure I shouldn't have to. Besides, I think about you all the time and it helps me detach from all of this. It releases me. When you look at life from far away enough, the things we talk, think, and gossip about fade to tiny dots, to nothing. I think, will this all matter in thirty years?

I will see my other lover, the painter, in a few weeks. None of us share continents, which makes things simple. I touch his face like it's holy. He likes to tell me that I'm free, that I can't be held in a cage, and I used to deny it. But one day I realized I don't tell him about the others because something about that really does keep me free. I love him, though, and it feels easy.

When I think of them and the love I hold for them, it unfurls into a greater love. My chest multiplies with it. I even want to hold the faces of my friends and tell them I love them. I don't feel trapped or anchored, which is really strange, Yshwa. I stop being afraid of relocations and I can move wherever I want because I know that I will be loved constantly across all space. And even if it fades with them, it will bloom again. We are all conduits. It moves through us freely.

Yshwa, I am tired of pain. It's just easier to focus on love and an existence outside this world. At least that feels like freedom.

Still, you like to send me new lovers, like impulsive presents. Like that one who I thought was going to be cocky and brash. He arrived after I had a difficult week and he turned out to be shy and clumsy, like a boy. He was single-minded in bed, his face serene and focused, his body hammering. Boys fuck like that, fast and hard and desperate. But when we stood on the open train platform, exposed to the sky, he pulled me to his chest. I turned my head away so my lipstick wouldn't stain his clothes and he kissed my forehead more times than anyone had in the past few years. He talked about tennis all the time, like Ewan used to. When we said good-bye, I was wearing the same dress he'd met me in.

"I'll miss you," I texted.

"You made my trip," he typed back.

Still, I am very lonely. They help me forget this, but sometimes it shows up like a continent shifting onto my chest. I'm so tired of being empty. I turned it inside out and wore it like a glove, smeared it on the walls until my house shouted *empty, empty,*

empty. I didn't know what to do with it afterward. All I know is that it hurts to be in the spaces between freedom.

"Can I have a hug?" I ask my white T-shirt lover.

"Of course," he answers, and holds me. "Are you okay?"

I want to tell him that my heartache is acting up again, but instead I smile and lie and lie next to his body, watching an animated movie flicker across the screen. I take a little comfort in the fact that he chose to be lying here with me. It matters, even though I still feel lonely with him there.

He saw the scars on my arms for the first time today.

"We have to talk," he said.

"I used to cut myself," I replied. "I stopped."

"I'm glad you stopped," he said, but it reminded me of how long all of this has been hurting. The pain is so old, Yshwa. I don't even have the strength to want anything anymore. I just float and stare at the sky, and when the pain hits, I arch my neck to keep the water from overcoming my face. Months ago, the painter looked at me as we lay in his bed.

"That sadness never really leaves your eyes," he said.

When I was out in Lagos with a group of friends, I met this Somali boy who told me I inhabit a space between depression and happiness, a sweet spot, a brilliant spot. I stared at him and wondered if it was true. If it was, could that spot be more real than either end of that spectrum? It would be a point of perfect balance, I thought.

"You are the most beautiful woman I have seen in all my life," he said.

“Why?” I asked.

He stared at me, then laughed. “Beauty is beauty,” he said, shaking his head. “It just is.”

I stared back at him. He hadn’t been able to stop drinking all night. He had worked his way through small glasses of tequila, larger glasses of vodka, occasional cups of tap water, and he was now holding a blue glass full of gin. I watched him and then I told him about Ewan. When I mentioned Donyen, his face changed.

“You’re too pretty to be gay,” he said.

Later that night, he asked if we had met in a previous life, and I said nothing. We all went to another club, and there, he took my hand and pulled me out under some purple lights.

“I will miss you,” he said. “I wish we had more time.”

I wasn’t sure what he was running away from, but I wanted to tell him that I was the wrong place to run to. It was impossible for me to love him. He had too much hate inside and he thought I would fall for words, as if you can get me with my own weapon. Try a god, I should have told him, they like when you run to them.

Honestly, Yshwa, I just want to rest. Let me find a place where even if I’m alone, I can sit on my veranda and look at a mango tree and we can just talk. You will be the words in my mouth and the ones that fall from my fingers; you will be the one to whom I direct my longing.

NZỌPỤTA

(Salvation)

Chapter Twenty

Hiding, oh, hiding! The hidden should hide very well,
because I am letting go the leopard.

We

Allow us a moment to explain a few things. When you break something, you must study the pattern of the shattering before you can piece it back together. So it was with the Ada. She was a question wrapped up in breath: How do you survive when they place a god inside your body? We said before that it was like shoving a sun into a bag of skin, so it should be no surprise that her skin would split or her mind would break. Consider her burned open. It was an unusual incarnation, to be a child of Ala as well as an ọgbanje, to be mothered by the god who owns life yet pulled toward death. We did the best we could.

Because we came through gates that did not close behind us, it was easy for us to make reality loose for the Ada. We had one foot on the other side at all times; it was nothing to step away from this world. And you must know this, you must see, how this world is a terrible and wicked place. We sectioned off the Ada in lavish and extravagant folds, playing fast with her memories. There are many advantages to a broken mind.

When the Ada was a child and the neighbor's son came into the room she shared with Añuli, when he reached his hand between the Ada's legs, under the cartoon nightgown she wore, we decided that she did not need to remember the exact ripplings of his fingers. Not that time, or the time after, or the time after that. It continued until the Ada wrote Chima a letter and asked him to stop inviting the neighbor's son over late at night, which was when it stopped. We sectioned off the image of his silhouette bending over her bed, of his arm reaching. When the neighbor himself, the boy's father, groped the Ada when he had her alone in his living room, when she was twelve, we did it again. We sectioned well—the Ada who was before the sectioning was not the same child after the sectioning. When she reached back for the memory, it would be as if it belonged to someone else, not her.

There was only us; we couldn't entrust her to anyone else. Saachi left and Saul was always at his hospital, and the Ada was at the whim of Chima's hands. He beat her often because he could—he was the first son and the firstborn, and she was his responsibility. The Ada fought back, and cried for her human mother until she realized that it made no difference. Even when Saachi did return, once or twice a year, it was not real. "She will leave," Chima reminded the Ada, when she tried to report him to Saachi, "and it will be just you and me again." By the time he raised a belt to her, the Ada knew no one would stay long enough to protect her.

When we were first placed inside her, with these humans, the odds were that the Ada would survive. It was, in retrospect, a very low bar to set. She did not die, yes, but she was not guarded, she was violated, so as far as we were concerned, they failed. This is why we have never regretted stepping in, whether as ourself or the beastself. Show us someone, anyone, who could have saved her better.

Sectioning the Ada gave her isolated pockets of memory, each containing a different version of her. There were versions to whom bad things had happened and, therefore, there were also versions of her to whom these things had not happened. The Ada could look back on her life and see, like clones, several of her standing there in a line. This terrified her, because if there were so many of her, then which one was she? Were they false and her current self real, or was her current self false and it was one of the others, lost in the line, who was the real Ada? We could not alleviate her terror because we would not allow a bridge between her and the past sections of her. We had separated them for a reason. Many things are better than a complete remembering; many things we do are a mercy.

But there were still dangers involved in what we did; sectioning is a brutal exercise, after all, and it became uncontrolled. The Ada was living in multiple realities at once, floating loosely between them, forgetting what each one felt like as soon as she moved to a new one. It was as if she had been thrown back into the open gates and was trapped forever between realms. For her it was deeply unsettling and felt like a developing madness. So the Ada started marking her skin in new ways, to remind herself of her past versions, tattooing her arms and wrists and legs. We accepted this because it was a worthy sacrifice; there is little difference between using a blade and this alternative, this ripping through the skin with multiple needles, injecting ink until the flesh swells and leaks and bleeds. She had a thick sleeve of black ink tattooed down her left forearm, where she usually did the blood offerings, and she never cut herself again after that. We had all evolved.

She even put a portrait of us on the high of her left arm, of herself staring out, of us peering over her shoulder with our mouth fastened to the junction of neck and trapezius, a phantom arm wrapping around her, a ring suspended in the blankness. All these things she was doing to her skin made her closer to us; it was like an advertisement, a timeline of sections, who she was on the inside being revealed on the outside. We have always been in support of that, like when we carved up her chest. Knowing that Ala, in her cruel motherlove, would not permit us to return through her mouth and into her womb, all we wanted now was wholeness. But when a thing has been created with deformations and mismatched edges, sometimes you have to break it some more before you can start putting it back together. And sometimes, when the thing is a god, you need someone holy for that.

Chapter Twenty-One

How can one tell the story of a rain that fell on him,
when he is ignorant of where the rain started falling on him?

We

It was good and correct that the Ada met the priest back in Nigeria; some things must happen on home soil if they are to happen at all. It was in Lagos, yes, not back in the Southeast where we were first born, but that was acceptable because the priest was Yoruba, and with these things, compromises must be made. He was a sound artist who lived in Paris, who had been away for fifteen years, who was pulled back just in time to meet us. He arrived like a torrent, so for this telling, let us call him Lẹshi.

Lẹshi was a thin man, tall and dark-skinned, with eyes lined in kohl and lashes stroked with mascara. He watched the Ada from the minute he first saw her, before her eyes found him, a private stretch of time. After they met, they moved cautiously around each other for the first day or so, wearing flesh faces but smelling the things under their respective skins. We were intrigued by him—he reeked of power, of in-between-ness, and he advertised it freely. The Ada's friends insisted that he must love men—no one, they said, would wear that much woman on their face otherwise. But we recognized the marks Lẹshi displayed; we knew that they told what spaces he lived in, those liminal gutters. We wanted to sit with him because he felt like how Ewan did the first time the Ada met him, that immediate click, that rightness with a faint promise of changing a life.

Out in the parking lot on the second night, Lẹshi and the Ada leaned against a car in the parking lot, away from the floodlights.

"Why don't you come back to the hotel with me?" he asked.

The Ada laughed and shook her head. He was a stranger, but she was not afraid because we knew him, something in his marrow matched ours. Still, she refused. "I don't want people to talk," she said.

Lẹshi looked at her, and his eyes were heavy and amused. "I can tell you now," he said. "You're going to come back with me."

He was not being arrogant. He wasn't human enough for that. The Ada hesitated, and Lẹshi tilted his head at her.

"Since when did you care what they think?" he said, and we stared at him through the Ada's eyes, then we laughed because he was right. None of this mattered. They were all human complications; they would die with time—everything always died. The Ada left with him, to the white nest of his hotel room, and it consumed her for the next two nights.

Lệshi's energy hummed against the walls and we fed on it, sealed inside a cocoon that rejected the city's reality.

"I felt you the minute you first walked into the room," he told the Ada as she curled up in an armchair. "So much power."

She blushed. "But I didn't even say anything. You all were rehearsing. I just walked in and sat down."

Lệshi smiled faintly. "Yes," he said. "Exactly. That's all you had to do and everyone knew you had entered the room."

Asụghara grinned. "Do you mind if I shower?" she asked, transparent as thin ice. We allowed it—to have the beastself show was inevitable, we would let her play. She stripped off the Ada's clothes and ran the water and the priest watched, still and relaxed. He did not touch her; he had a lover back in Paris. Asụghara prowled and purred because she didn't care; humans were predictable, full of hunger and terrible at restraint. But as we were learning, the priest was not human, and so he smiled, immune to her bait, then coaxed and petted her until she gave in and laid her head on his thighs, naked and docile, the Ada's body strewn over his sheets. Lệshi remained fully dressed for the two nights, keeping his head covered. Perhaps he knew what damage Asụghara could cause if he let her against his skin.

"I can see you change," he told us, his eyes narrowed in interest. "Your body language. How you talk. Your eyes. You're not always the same person, are you?"

Understand this if you understand nothing: it is a powerful thing to be seen. We found ourself venturing timidly from the Ada's mouth, telling him about us, how we were a misplaced god, how we were not human, how we had divided the Ada's mind. Lẹshi looked at the Ada in soft awe—even a priest can be ministered to.

"I've always felt like that," he said, "my whole life, but I've never been able to articulate it the way you just did."

The Ada showed him her blackened forearm and the soft raised scars that the ink was covering. The priest ran his fingers over it, then rolled up his shirtsleeve to show her his own. It covered his whole forearm—puckered, shiny flesh seized up in a keloid. "They reconstructed it," he told her. He had been performing; he had dug out the flesh himself and fed it to the crowd. We understood. It is like we said: when gods awaken in you, sometimes you carve yourself up to satisfy them.

"I want you to last forever," she whispered to him, their faces mirroring each other's in the pillows. We ran her fingers over the skin of his cheek and his eyes shuddered close.

"Please," he whispered back. "You have to stop that." He had a lover already; we were not allowed to touch him too much.

We cannot tell you the whole of it, the parts that do not fit into words, the parts that we have already sectioned away for safekeeping. When gods are talking, eavesdroppers will be struck deaf. Be satisfied with this: Lẹshi told the Ada truths. He read her and prophesied and tested her, tested us. *What are your fears? Why are you doing this? No, that is a lie. Try again. That is also a lie. Stop being afraid. Yes, now you are telling the truth. Do you see? When you say this, what are you trying to mold? Here is the edge of a cliff, do you have the liver to stand there? You should, you stink of power. No, you cannot hold my hand. I am not yours, I am not really here. You have to stand alone, none of this works if you do not stand alone. I see you. I won't touch you, but I see you. Try it again.*

And just like that, in two nights with the moon shifting slowly between phases, he reached inside us, through us, and he pulled the Ada out into the light. Believe, we would have kept her inside our great shadow, but Lẹshi pushed himself into her terrible loneliness, called her by all of our names, then left, because some gates do close. The only time he kissed her was on the morning of his leaving, and when he was gone, we were bereft.

Ah, we have always claimed to rule the Ada, but here is the truth: she was easier to control when she thought she was weak. Here is another truth: she is not ours, we are hers. We did not know who sent the priest to remind her (most likely it was our brothersisters) and we wanted to be angry, but Lẹshi had been a pit of beauty and we couldn't find enough anger to keep us afloat. Instead we let ourself sink into him, into the space his absence had created. We relived the two nights over and over; we plastered his face all over the marble and wept at the loss of his voice. When the sadness seemed like it might fade, we regurgitated it and rolled it, tragic and beautiful, around the Ada's teeth. We did not section him, even though the mere thought of his face was heartbreak.

The mourning of him became a ritual in and of itself, a dramatic enactment of sorrow. The Ada stumbled around, blinded by memory. When you have been hiding in a great shadow, it hurts to look at the light, to be awake, to feel.

"I wish I had filmed him," she told Añuli. We wanted to project him against a wall and play it on a loop, to watch his jaw turn toward us a thousand times, until the electricity finished, until our eyes collapsed.

"He's not coming back," Añuli said bluntly. She was being kind, but we already knew he would not return; we had felt the reverberation when he left. It was cruel, it was unfair! Skins are not meant to shed so quickly—it was as if he had hooked his fingers into our eyes and flayed us neatly, peeling us raw. Who we were before Lẹshi laid his long hands on us was not who we were afterward. No, afterward we were done. We were ready to stop the births and the namings—the Ada was ready to take her own front.

When we fell back, it tasted like a kind of death. But as the Ada moved out of our shadow and into her body, we found ourself watching her with a grim pride. She was scarred, yes, gouged in places even. But she was—she has always been—a terrifyingly beautiful thing. If you ever saw her at her fullest, you would understand—power becomes the child. She is heavy and unbearably light, still her mother's hatchling. Think of her when the moon is rich, flatulent, bursting with pus and light, repugnant with strength.

Yes, now you are beginning to understand.

Chapter Twenty-Two

The masquerade has moved into the arena. You will be flogged if you remain. Your ears will be filled with news if you run away.

Ada

We have a saying back home: Ịchụrụ chi ya aka mgba. One does not challenge their chi to a wrestling match. It feels as if that's what I've been doing for years now, wrestling as if it could end in anything other than my loss. But it's a relief to finally be thrown, to lie with my back on the sand, alive and out of breath. You can see the sky properly this way. Besides, the sand is my mother and no one can run from her. They say that she can find you as long as your feet are touching the earth, and once she does, the earth can split open like a pod and just swallow you up. There's a story about a man called Alụ who tried to escape her by jumping from tree to tree like a monkey. He lived like that for years, floating in the treetops, and when Ala couldn't find him, she haunted the whole forest. His name became the word for taboo, and all taboos are committed against her. Gods really do take things personally.

I wish I could say that after Lẹshi, I became an obedient child who listened to my first mother and walked with my brother-sisters, but I was too stubborn and I was still afraid. I know how mad it sounds to call yourself a god. Believe me, I fought it at first. Let me ask questions, I thought, and so I ended up in a restaurant in Lagos speaking to an Igbo man, a historian. When I told him about my others and my name and my first mother, he leaned over.

"I cannot talk to you about these things in an air-conditioned restaurant in Lagos," he said. "You understand? But you are on the right path. This journey is the right thing to do."

It should have been reassuring, but it only terrified me further. I wanted to stop there, but I couldn't, because this was my life, you understand? No matter how mad it sounded, the things that were happening in my head were real and had been happening for a very long time. After all the doctors and the diagnoses and the hospitals, this thing of being an ọgbanje, a child of Ala—that was the only path that brought me any peace. So yes, I was terrified, but I went back to talk to the historian again.

"The name that was given to you has many connotations, you hear?" He wore glasses and spoke in a rush of words. "The python's egg means a precious child. A child of the gods, or the deity themself. The experiences you've had suggest that there is a spiritual connection, which you need to go and learn about. Your journey will not be complete until you do that."

He leaned back and folded his arms. "There is nothing more anybody can tell you. It's important for you to understand your place on this earth."

Sometimes, you recognize truth because it destroys you for a bit. I fell apart that night, crying uncontrollably, throwing my phone against a wall and hyperventilating until everything around me started to fade. I was at a lover's house, the painter, and he put his arm around me, holding me up.

"Stay with me," he said urgently. "Stay with me, Ada."

I was gone, inside my head, and I turned to my others. *What does he mean,* I asked. *I'm not going anywhere.*

They frowned. *We're not sure. Even if you faint, you'll wake up.*

"Stay with me, please," he begged.

He doesn't know what to do, I told them, and they nodded.

Something has to be done, they said. *Pick one of us.*

I looked at them and it was the same as looking at myself. *Asụghara,* I said. She was older now, less brutal but still efficient. When she stepped forward, I stopped crying.

"I need to call my mother," she said, using my mouth. I was already learning what this new balance could feel like, where I controlled how we moved. More and more, I realized how useless it had been to try and become a singular entity.

"Won't your mother be worried?" the painter asked.

Asụghara shook our head. His mother would panic, but Saachi was different, she was a selected human. She wasn't the type to fall apart just like that. When she picked up the phone, Asụghara spoke between my gasps for air and kept her voice level. "I'm having a panic attack and I don't know what to do. Hyperventilating. Feel like I'm about to faint."

Saachi replied with matching calm, her voice focused. "Have you eaten today?"

"No."

"Your blood sugar is low. Where are you?"

"At a friend's house."

"Okay. You need to lie down, but first you have to eat or drink something. Right now, understand?"

I was drifting too fast. It took Asụghara a few moments to find my mouth again, and when she spoke, our voice was faint. "I don't know."

Another mother might have let worry show in her voice, but Saachi had nearly had me die on her. This was nothing in comparison. "Is your friend there?" she asked.

"Yes. You want to talk to him?"

"Yes, put him on the phone."

Asụghara handed the phone to the painter and fell back into the marble. It was too much to sustain, keeping a functional self in front. I could hear the painter's voice as he spoke to Saachi, his tone anxious and respectful. After he hung up, he brought me a glass of water and watched me as I sipped it.

"What do you want to eat?" he asked.

Asụghara tried one last time. "I should lie down," we said, but when I tried to stand, my legs were nothing. I couldn't walk; my body was too far away. I started crying again and the painter picked me up and carried me to his bedroom. When he put me down on the bed, the hard foam of the mattress felt like ground. I turned on my side and pressed my cheek to it. The skirt I was wearing fanned out over the bed and cinched at my waist.

"Breathe," he was saying, bringing his face close to mine. His hand was on my skin. "Breathe."

It felt so much easier not to. It seemed outrageous to expect my body to put in that much effort just to draw in air. For what?

Just stop, my others suggested. *You could just stop breathing. It feels so easy.*

They were right, it did. I held my breath, but it didn't feel like I was holding my breath, it felt like there should never have been breath. It felt like the entire concept of breath had been something I imagined. After all, my body was never meant to move like this. These lungs had to have been built for show. They should never have expanded and I should never have been alive.

The painter shook me, but my eyes felt heavier than cold mud. I fumbled to unzip the side of my skirt and the pressure on my diaphragm eased, but I was still drifting. It wasn't until he put a cold towel on the back of my neck that the gray moved away, almost reluctantly. The fading stopped and I fell asleep.

The next morning, I was back in my body and the painter was relieved.

"It's one thing to talk about your spiritual matters," he said. He knew about the sections of my mind, my tongue and scales. "It's another thing to see it."

I was confused. "What do you mean?"

He gave me a look. "Come on, Ada. You almost went to the other side last night." I scoffed but he was serious. "That's why I kept telling you to stay."

"I would have come back," I said.

He shook his head and I could see residual worry on his face. "You don't know that."

I fell silent. Maybe he had a point.

"And you know what was the scariest part?" he continued. "I looked into your eyes and you weren't afraid. You knew you were slipping away but you had peace in your eyes."

I kept listening, and he searched my face from the pillow next to me.

"It's like your people were calling you and you were listening to them. So I kept telling you to stay."

I smiled to reassure him and touched his cheek. "Thank you," I said. I couldn't remember the last time anyone had been afraid for me. I also knew it wasn't by chance that this had happened while I was looking for answers to these questions I was afraid of. The historian was right—there was nothing else anyone could tell me.

I knew the brothersisters hadn't been serious about trying to drag me over to the other side the night before. The thing about Ala is that you don't move against her. If she turned me back from the gates and told me to live, then I would have to live, ọgbanje or not. Even the brothersisters weren't reckless enough to try and disobey her, which meant that they were just trying to scare me, or warn me. It sounded like the kind of thing they would do. If the wooden gong gets too loud, you tell it the wood it was carved from.

But like I said, I'm stubborn. I didn't go to find Ala, not on that trip. I went back to America and called Malena and told her what happened. She agreed with the historian.

"You need to really know your roots, mi amor," she said. "It's a long journey, but once you get that started, you'll feel much better. It's difficult because you don't really know what you're getting yourself into when you make your commitment with them, and it's difficult because they're overprotective of us. But you'll have a better sense of self." She paused. "You know how old you are? You're older than me, Ada. Spiritually, you're older than me. You're sixteen thousand years old. Because of who you are, because of who you're born into. You have a different name. You're wiser. You just need guidance."

She sounded like a prophet, like someone was speaking through her mouth again.

I decided to start small, with prayer. The first night I tried it was because my mind was spinning out like it sometimes does, loud and uncontrolled. I was so tired. They were pulling at my thoughts, all of them. Sometimes I don't draw a line between my others and the brothersisters; they're all ọgbanje after all, siblings to each other more than to me. But I was so tired. How many years had I spent trying to balance them, trying to kill them, defending against their retaliations, bribing them, starving and begging them? I used to try praying to Yshwa, but it's like he has no effect on them. I can see why Asụghara thought he was useless.

So that night, I prayed to Ala. I didn't want to do it in English even though I knew she would understand; language is only a human thing. Igbo had always been stunted coming from me, but there was one word that was easy, that slipped from my tongue like salted palm oil and tasted correct.

"Nne," I said, and the word was double-jointed. Mother.

I felt her immediately and the brothersisters lifted off my mind in a hurried cloud. I was cast into a vast, empty space and everything around me was peaceful. It felt like the otherworld—that's how I knew that I was inside her, suspended and rocked.

Find your tail, she told me, and her words slithered. They were silver and cool.

Her voice came with meaning. I had forgotten that if she is a python, then so am I. If I don't know where my tail is, then I don't know anything. I don't know where I'm going, I don't know where the ground is, or where the sky is, or if I'm pointing away from my head. The meaning was clear. Curve in on yourself. Touch your tongue to your tail so you know where it is. You will form the inevitable circle, the beginning that is the end. This immortal space is who and where you are, shapeshifter. Everything is shedding and everything is resurrection.

The second time I called her, she said nothing. She just took me and put me inside a calabash. I was tiny like a hatchling, lying against the curve and feeling the fibers beneath me. I was curled up. I was so small and she was wrapped around the outside of the calabash, her scales pressed against the neck. No one would touch it once they saw that she held it, which meant that no one would touch me.

It is hard to ignore a god's voice, especially one like hers. The message was so simple; I couldn't pretend not to hear it. *Come home,* my brothersisters sang. *Come home and we will stop looking for your trouble.* I bent my neck and raised my hands and submitted. What else was there to do? You cannot wrestle with your chi and win. In this new obedience, I decided to go back to Umuahia and see my first mother. I knew it would be impossible to close the gates, but I was the bridge, so it did not matter. If I was anything else, maybe I would've been uncertain and full of questions, looking for mediators or trying to speak to my ancestors. But I had surrendered and the reward was that I knew myself. I did not come from a human lineage and I will not leave one behind. I have no ancestors. There will be no mediators. How can, when my brothersisters speak directly to me, when my mother answers when I call her?

Like the historian said, you have to know your place on this earth. It was very hard, letting go of being human. I felt as if I had been taken away from the world I knew, like there was now thick glass between me and the people I loved. If I told them the truth, they would think I was mad. It was difficult to accept not being human but still being contained in a human body. For that one, though, the secret was in the situation. Ọgbanje are as liminal as is possible—spirit and human, both and neither. I am here and not here, real and not real, energy pushed into skin and bone. I am my others; we are one and we are many. Everything gets clearer with each day, as long as I listen. With each morning, I am less afraid.

My mother draws closer now. I can see a red road opening before me; the forest is green on either side of it and the sky is blue above it. The sun is hot on the back of my neck. The river is full of my scales. With each step, I am less afraid. I am the brothersister who remained. I am a village full of faces and a compound full of bones, translucent thousands. Why should I be afraid? I am the source of the spring.

All freshwater comes out of my mouth.

Acknowledgments

From the very beginning.

Enuma Okoro, for saying to me in a restaurant in Providence, "Oh, you *have* to write the spiritual book first!" For your friendship and the feedback on early chapters. The painter, for tenderness and having my back when I started on this path. The priest, for breaking me. The historian, Ed Keazor, thank you a thousand times over for being there.

Tiona McClodden, for every moment of your unflinching and active belief in my work, for inspiring me with yours. For the multiple ways you saw and supported me, for teaching me rigor. Christi Cartwright, for being an excellent and meticulous reader. For always coming through with the industry insight and being my friend. Dana Spiotta and Chris Kennedy, for the first draft feedback. The Creative Writing MFA Program at Syracuse University, for funding me during the year in which I wrote the book. The Callaloo Creative Writing Workshop where the book concept solidified and the Caine Prize Writing Workshop where I finished the first draft. Cave Canem, for the poetry workshops in which I wrote Chapter 15.

Chimamanda Adichie, for the Farafina Creative Writing Workshop and the ripples from that. For that moment when I started to tell you about the book and you tilted your head, looked at me, and said, "Ah, so you're an ọgbanje."

Binyavanga Wainaina, for making me cancel my Uber to talk about the work. For being such a staunch champion of this book and making sure it was taken care of. You believed in it so much that I did too.

To Eloghosa Osunde and Nana Nyarko Boateng, for reading the manuscript and giving me reasons why this work matters, for always seeing and loving me. Isaac Otidi Amuke, with all my love. You know why. Sarah Chalfant, Jackie Ko, and Alba Ziegler-Bailey at the Wylie Agency, for being amazing. My brilliant editor, Peter Blackstock, for believing.

My mother, June, for letting me interview her and my little twin sister, Yagazie, for that time when I was freaking out about what I needed to believe in order to write this book and you told me to treat it like I was a method actor, to surrender. So I went in and never came back out, which was perfect. Also, for everything else. Thank you.

The lovebears and squad, for being my community and chosen family. We all we got.

Bobbi, mi hermana mi amor, thank you for everything. And always, my darling Rachel, for all these years of fierce and unwavering love.

Read on for an essay by
Akwaeke Emezi,
which first appeared on *BuzzFeed READER*
on February 7, 2018.

Writing into the Unknown

My childhood can be measured easily, in pools of light spilling onto pages and books blanketing the surfaces of our house in Aba, Nigeria. When the electricity died, as it often did, I read by candlelight or with a flashlight balanced against my body. Both my parents had been heavy readers; they dragged their libraries into their marriage and kept them separate, distinct. My father had a collection of Reader's Digest condensed novels on the top shelf of the bookcase in my brother's room, and in one of them, a little boy called his sister stupid because she was seven. I took it personally when I first read it, bristling with rage because she and I were the same age then—seven didn't mean we were stupid.

When my parents discovered I'd started reading the sex advice columns in my mother's magazines as a child because I had run out of material, they quickly bought me more books.

Stories became my entire world, unchecked and unrestricted; I was nine when I read V.C. Andrews' *Flowers in the Attic*. My sister and I rummaged through my mother's trunk, a steel tomb tucked in a corner of the house, and we found a copy of Daphne du Maurier's *Rebecca*, with that haunting first line—"*Last night I dreamt I went to Manderley again*." My father's library had a copy of Ken Follett's book *The Key to Rebecca*, which I'd read before, and eleven-year-old me was in awe at finding a book that I'd first read about inside another book; worlds eating worlds, all made by words.

By the time I started college in the States, I'd read every book in my childhood home. The white dean of my school kept introducing me as the sixteen-year-old freshman from West Africa who'd already read Dickens and Tolstoy and Dostoevsky, as if any of that was meant to be surprising or special. I'd only read those books because they were there; the awe associated with a certain European literary canon wasn't relevant. I'd also read Cyprian Ekwensi, Ayi Kwei Armah, Buchi Emecheta, Chinua Achebe, the secret copy of *The Joy of Sex* hidden away in my parents' room, every encyclopedia entry in my school library on Greek mythology, labels on shampoo bottles, the sides of cornflake boxes and Bournvita tins during breakfast, countless contraband Harlequin and Mills & Boon romance novels bartered with secondary school classmates, narrative interludes in my brother's video games, and all the parts of the Bible that referenced sex. It wasn't until much later that I realized there was a canon I was "expected" to prioritize, especially if I wanted to consider myself a writer, that the work of dead white men could be a type of currency.

A few years ago, during a nonfiction workshop in upstate New York, I read Vladimir Nabokov for the first time. The workshop was mostly white, except for myself and two other writers of color, and we'd been assigned his memoir, *Speak, Memory*. I hadn't expected much before reading the book, but I ended up delightfully surprised at how strongly it resonated: the ways in which Nabokov engaged with his own selfhood, the thinking that unspooled from that, how it reflected what I was doing in the debut novel I was working on. I felt like I'd found some precedent for what I was creating, precedent that had been difficult to find in the work of people who looked like me.

On the day the workshop met, we were all meant to bring in pieces we'd written to be critiqued after we discussed the assigned reading. I brought the requested printout of my work, as did all the white writers, but the other two writers of color had nothing to turn in.

"It's Nabokov," they said. "No one writes like he does, no one can do what he does." They were so intimidated by his brilliance that they'd chosen not to present their own work. I didn't know how to respond, but my enthusiasm about the connection I'd felt with his work dimmed into a guarded wariness. In the air of that room, as everyone agreed with them about how untouchable Nabokov was, it felt as if the only permitted emotion was awe, like anything else would be seen as incredibly arrogant. I wasn't supposed to read Nabokov and think, "Ah, we're doing something similar with this study of the self." I was off script; I was supposed to be intimidated, worshipful.

I figured they knew better. They'd read more than I had; I was clumsy and naive to read Nabokov and feel like maybe I'd found a peer. As a young writer working on her first book, it made me even more nervous about what I was writing, the ways my work deviated from other stories that were out there. I was besieged with anxieties: What if I wasn't allowed to do what I was doing? What if it didn't get published? What if the gatekeepers read it and saw it as arrogant, me stepping out of place, writing about metaphysical selves as if I had the creative freedom of a white writer in this industry? I knew the world saw me as a black writer, as an African woman, and I'd read enough about racism in publishing to worry about how it could play out in real time against me.

I kept looking for stories like the one I was telling, but I couldn't find them, and that terrified me. Maybe I was meant to be writing stories that looked more like what popular African writers had done before; maybe if I stuck to themes that were familiar, perhaps even expected, I could have some of the success they had. I couldn't blame the other writers of color in my workshop for swallowing their work instead of presenting it. They were hearing the same message, broadcast by the limited range of our stories made available to us, a message that seemed to tell us which of these stories would be allowed through the gates and which would be held back. "When you read work like Nabokov's," the message hissed, "turn your face away. That's not the kind of work you can make. There's a script for people like you; stick to it."

I've been a reader all my life; I know books can be many things. Some are manuals, some are informational pamphlets, some are reportage. Some are portals into other constructed worlds, a favorite from my childhood and the root of my deep love for speculative fiction. Some are windows into another's experiences, or even into our own—our raging desires to be seen and to see ourselves show in this. I wonder if it is enough, this reflection of known things.

As I clawed my way through my manuscript, I remained deeply doubtful about its future. It went out on submission and none of the rejections surprised me. I'd prepared myself for them — not because of the writing, per se, but just in terms of the market. The book wasn't "immigrant experience" enough; so much of it was internal—wouldn't it be difficult to sell a book so deeply rooted in Igbo ontology to a US audience? I occasionally talk about placelessness as it attaches to myself and my life, but in that fog of worry, it felt as if it had extended to my book, wrapping it in blurry tentacles. Months later, while composing a description of it with my editor and agent, the word "identity" came up.

"We can't use that word as is," I wrote in an email. "Everyone's going to assume that we mean national or racial identity just because I'm a Nigerian writer. We have to specify that it's about metaphysical identity."

"Are you sure you want to use the word metaphysical?" they asked.

"I know it might sound pretentious, but I honestly don't know another accurate word," I wrote back.

My main character's life and experiences weren't centered on her being African, or black, or an immigrant—those were negligible, secondary. Her core conflict was that she was embodied: that she existed, that she had selves, that she was several. I didn't know any other books by African writers that asked or answered the questions I was working with, but I very much wanted to find precedent. I figured that would tell me if what I was doing was permissible or possible, that it would allow me to predict the trajectory of the book and afford me some security. Sometimes we don't get the reassurances we want; we make the work anyway. By then, I knew what it was like to look for books that reflected my world and not be able to find them. I know the power of people feeling seen, having access to stories that mirror their own, and what it moves inside them.

I wonder if it's enough; I know, for me, it's not.

It is summer in New York and I am at a cathedral uptown, meeting with Katherine Agard, a Trinidadian writer whose work and mind I love. We walk past the ceiling that looks like nothingness and climb into the ornate choir section. I give her a signed advance copy of my book and she gives me a spray of velvet orange flowers. We eat two tangerines, piling the rinds sweetly around us. Katherine is telling me about her book and its strangeness, how she's not sure it is actually a book; we are thinking about what a book can be. I tell her how I want reflections that are alive, that shift things for me instead of showing me the familiar. Perhaps it's because I couldn't find my own world when I looked for it in books, and though I found other worlds—the ones I've lived in, pretended in, moved through—it felt different, but not enough.

So I turned instead to work that didn't reflect my story, but made me want to write new ones. I fell for books that challenged form and convention because something in them challenged me. Within the cathedral's quiet, I tell Katherine about Alain Mabanckou's *Broken Glass*, punctuated with commas alone, and Helen Oyeyemi's *Mr. Fox*, storytelling within storytelling, blurred realities. I pull up the e-book of Fran Ross's 1974 novel, *Oreo*, on my phone and show her the first two pages, with the diagrams and the equations, the magnificent things Ross did with structure. "*That's* an alive reflection," I say. "It's the kind of work you'd think only white writers get to make."

Katherine picks up what I'm saying about inert reflections. "They're not reformulating anything," she says. "They're transporting between ideas that already exist, nothing is being shaped from the unknown into . . . well, something that is still unknown, really. Alive reflections are writing into the unknown."

I imagine it as casting out into unformed space, tracing blindly, discovering something by the writing of it. I'd started my book because I had a slew of questions about existence that I was trying to figure out, rooting the process in Igbo reality and my own archive, but I'd continued with it because it was also a reflection for those of us living in shifting realities, worlds framed as madness, bordered by unknowns. To write into that space was the only way I knew how to confront it, how to start wrangling a semblance of peace through the storm I'd been hiding in my head, and nothing has surprised me more than having the resulting book be read and received well. It allows me a wary hope that space will be made for writers of color working in the experimental, that we'll get to see more and more of our own books, showing us we can tell all kinds of stories and write whatever reflections we want. We don't have to swallow our work or be afraid that it's too deviant to do well; there is, in fact, no canon we cannot touch. Even when seized by a thousand fears, we can make strange and wonderful things simply for the sake of the strange and the wonderful, we can create without permission, we can write into the unknown.